THE BOOK OF BRADFORD

EDITED BY
SAIMA MIR

*For the remarkable and resilient folk of Bradford,
may the world know and love you as I do.*

First published in Great Britain in 2025 by Comma Press.
www.commapress.co.uk

Copyright © remains with the authors, editors, and Comma Press, 2025.
All rights reserved.
'Smoke of the Tide' copyright of the Literary Estate of Malachi Whitaker,
reproduced by permission of the Estate's Executor, Valerie Waterhouse.

'Bouncing Back' was first published in *In This Block There Lives a Slag... And Other Yorkshire Fables* (HarperCollins, 2001). 'Smoke of the Tide' was first published in *Frost in April* (Jonathan Cape, 1929). The names, characters and incidents portrayed in these works of fiction are entirely the work of the authors' imagination. Any resemblance to actual persons, living or dead, events, organisations or localities, is entirely coincidental. Any characters that appear, or claim to be based on real ones, are intended to be entirely fictional. The opinions of the authors are not those of the publisher.

The moral rights of the authors to be identified as the author of this Work have been asserted in accordance with the Copyright Designs and Patents Act 1988.

A CIP catalogue record of this book is available from the British Library.

ISBN-10: 1917093004
ISBN-13: 978-1917093002

Commissioned by Bradford 2025 UK City of Culture.

The publisher gratefully acknowledges the support of Arts Council England.

Printed and bound in England by CPI Antony Row Ltd.

Contents

INTRODUCTION Saima Mir	v
THE WICKEDEST MAN IN THE WORLD David Barnett	1
SMOKE OF THE TIDE Malachi Whitaker	19
SAMOSAS AND PARKIN Abda Khan	27
FIRE NEXT TIME Marcia Hutchinson	37
BOUNCING BACK Bill Broady	47
MADAM DOCTOR AND THE TEA LADY Sairish Hussain	79
ONE OF OUR OWN Ross Raisin	103
AROMA. TASTE. SWEET. CENTRE. Nick Ahad	119

CONTENTS

THE HOMECOMING Lesley McEvoy	137
THE ENDS M.Y. Alam	149
THE HOLE IN THE HEART Becky Cherriman	167
ABOUT THE CONTRIBUTORS	177

Introduction

BRADFORD IS A SOURCE of intrigue to those who don't know my home city, and I'm often asked to describe her on panels and in interviews – most recently by the presenter of BBC Radio 4's *Front Row*, Nick Ahad, who happens to be one of the authors in this anthology. We were discussing the 2025 UK City of Culture win, a designation that would ultimately lead, among other things, to this book. Nick and I have known each other for over twenty years and, as children of the city, she holds a great place in both our hearts. I told him Bradford, for me, is like an ageing duchess, fallen on hard times and I heard a sharp intake of breath.

As a novelist I try to write complicated women, females who are misunderstood and maligned, but who only ever want the best for their people.

Although I don't mention her by name, Bradford is very much the backdrop of my work. Dismissed, caricatured, and often reduced to clickbait, she has been branded as failing, as lost, and a place of division for too long.

To me, and the authors of these stories, she is none of these things, and the best thing about this great city is that she cares little for the shallow opinions of outsiders.

She has endured fires, floods, riots, closures, recessions, prejudice, neglect, and each time, she has risen, and we are witnessing this rise again.

INTRODUCTION

To know Bradford is to love her contradictions. That ageing duchess, who was once the belle of the ball, has known what it is to be adored, to stand at the centre of the world's gaze. Her mills once clothed empires in shades of velvet and wool, as she held the title of the Wool Capital of the World. That honour stemmed from the city's significant role in industry during the Industrial Revolution. At its peak, Bradford processed an estimated two-thirds of the nation's wool.

As a result, wealthy merchants built grand houses out of shimmering Yorkshire stone in places like Manningham and Heaton; buildings we now know as Cartwright Hall Art Gallery in the centre of Lister Park, or the lecture rooms of Victoria Hall, not to mention the schools and homes of workers of the people of Saltaire.

Bradford's name was spoken with reverence, and she was celebrated, but then came decline. As fortunes were lost, those imposing houses were left tired, and her reputation was tarnished, but, with hard times comes wisdom, and this is something the city has never lost. Along with courage, Bradford wears her history like pearls: each layer formed under pressure, each one gleaming.

Bradford is like my mother. She raised me, and for better or for worse, she is the voice in my head. I can say whatever I like about her but won't allow others to speak ill. That is, unless, like the writers in this book, they were also raised by this great city.

Because Bradford does that, she raises people and shapes them.

She takes us in her hands like clay, kneading us with tenderness, salting us with grit, and sends us out into the world resilient. It is important and necessary because coming from a place that is not always celebrated is hard, and it can break you. But the thing about struggle is that it makes men out of boys, women out of girls, and artists out of all of us.

INTRODUCTION

The city is the reason I am a writer, and every aspect of my work has Bradford at its bedrock.

Bradford nudges people along paths they could never have imagined. Whilst money and opportunity make success easier, it is handling conflict and contradiction that makes great art, music, and storytelling, and it is this that gives people the courage to push through and stay the course as they build enterprise and business.

From David Hockney to Steven Frayne, Zayn Malik to Heather Peace, A A Dhand to Liz Mistry, Bradford produces people who are restless, resilient, and remarkable. She does not give us an easy road, but she gives us fire in our bellies, and that fire carries us out into the world.

No one who comes here leaves the city unchanged, and although some may moan at first, when you scratch the surface you will always find a fondness for the place.

Whether you are born into the arms of the midwives of the Royal Infirmary, or arrive by chance or choice, disembarking at the Interchange or coming off the M606, the city marks you. Bradford seeps into your bones, and sharpens your sense of injustice, and bleeds into the way you see the world.

We, the people of this city, have long been truth-tellers. From the Brontës scribbling social truths after long walks along the moors, to authors tapping on laptops in the café mezzanine of the Wool Exchange-turned-Waterstones, or the ordinary folk who are the backbone of the district, speaking plainly on Manningham Lane, there is little appetite for pretence here. We are 'published and be damned' folk.

'Instagram keeps telling me I might be neurodiverse, because I can't not speak the truth,' I say to film director Dominic Leclerc, over coffee at the Media Museum. He laughs. 'But really, I think I'm just from Bradford!' I add.

He laughed in recognition, at the statement and our newly discovered connection. He is a successful theatre and TV director, a son of the city, having worked on the final series of

Sex Education. His mother had once taught at my school, and our connection is a reminder of Bradford's paradox. Despite being the fifth largest metropolitan district in England and Wales, somehow it can still feel like a village where we all know one another's stories.

Bradford has always been a city of dreamers, of visionaries, of people who grasp the invisible and drag it into reality. The mill owners who built that textile empire did so with grit and steam. They are now buried under the opulent and gaudy monuments that fill Undercliffe Cemetery, but the place is favoured by film folk from across the country. You can catch Tommy Shelby striding through the undergrowth of the cemetery in *Peaky Blinders*, or dining in the hallways of City Hall.

As well as the architectural gems, the textile industry brought with it migrants. German-Jewish, Irish, Polish, and then South Asian people flocked to the district for work. They carried with them flavours, music, languages, and faiths, and planted them into the northern soil until they bloomed.

Diversity of thought can bring with it friction but it greatly enhances creativity, and makes people who are better equipped to address complex challenges with innovative answers, and so make more informed decisions.

This anthology reflects that diversity.

As a cub reporter for *The Telegraph & Argus*, the newsroom in the centre of Bradford was a place of wonder for me. Daily editions piled high on desks, the scent of warm newsprint and ink in the air, it felt like stepping into the city's beating heart. The building itself, opened in the 1980s, was all dark glass, reflecting the city back at itself, while letting passersby peer into its hive of stories.

David Barnett, then features editor at the local paper, opened the door to my own journalistic career.

Years later, as I read his story of Aleister Crowley's strange arrival in Bradford in 1905 to seek out his disciples, it feels like

INTRODUCTION

a wink from the universe. Only days before, I had stumbled across a copy of Crowley's book in a TK Maxx in south-west London, the first time I'd seen his name since the 1990s, when friends and I whispered it over ghost stories at St Joseph's College on Cunliffe Road. Bradford makes those threads, weaving past into present in unexpected ways.

This book is stitched together from the same kind of synchronicities. Lesley McEvoy writes of a daughter scattering her father's ashes at Bolling Hall, finding solace in a stranger. The physical act of coming back to Bradford becomes symbolic of reconciling memory, migration and family ties. Her story echoes our own friendship. We met long before either of us were published, when I interviewed her for the BBC. A decade apart in age, different in race and religion, and yet instantly kindred spirits. Bradford has a way of doing that.

Nick Ahad takes us into the Sweet Centre, home of halwa puri, where sons confide in fathers and the aroma of spiced ghee carries memory as surely as it carries flavour. These are the moments that make a city: not just bricks and mills, but kitchens, streets, silences, and the invisible bonds between people. It is also the thing that those of us who move away, miss the most.

Bradford has always dared to look beyond the horizon, to reach for more. You see that dreaming in her very landscape. Drive down Lilycroft Road toward Manningham Lane: on the left, Lister's grand Yorkshire stone mill, imposing and magnificent; ahead, the green valley unspooling like ribbon.

In 'The Ends', when M.Y. Alam writes about the villas, crescents and squares 'reserved for the daddies who ran the city some hundred and some years ago', I know exactly which streets he's talking about. The city, like his story, is dramatic, contradictory, and surprising.

Yet too often, the headlines miss this. They miss the kind of camaraderie of which Sairish Hussain speaks in 'Madam Doctor and the Tea Lady'. They know nothing of how the sun

INTRODUCTION

hits the Bradford Royal Infirmary on a summer's day, or the exact hue of the foliage that grows across the roads.

When they linger on riots and burning cars, rehearsing Bradford's challenges and hardships like a tired chorus. They ignore the kind of shared generational sisterhood that Abda Khan's 'Samosas and Parkin' speaks of. It was the kind of connection that unfolded in the terraced and back-to-back houses of the sixties. The swapping of kind words and recipes, that developed into a love of food that made Bradford a curry capital, and created businesses that spread to the sprawling industrial estates that both surround and sit within the city.

Outsiders overlook the sweep of moors where the Brontës walked. Remember, these were Bradfordian women whose dramatised stories pulled in actors like Laurence Olivier, David Niven, Dilip Kumar, and now Margot Robbie, and who over a century later spawned a pop song that hundreds of us belted into our hairbrushes, channelling our inner Kate Bush as we called to Heathcliffe.

Our valleys that once powered the looms of thousands of machinists and weavers, also powered great art. The terraced streets from Girlington to Saltaire still hum with memory. Those who never get to know the city miss out on the beauty that lives here, as stubborn and enduring as the people who walk these streets. Streets that Ross Raisin's characters walk on their way to Valley Parade in 'One of Our Own'. Although this book comes 40 years after the tragedy that took the lives of 56 Bradford City fans, the events feel like they happened only yesterday. My father and younger brother were at that match, and I still remember my dad coming home only to lie down on the living room floor, trying to process what he'd witnessed.

Those devastating events of 1985 are also alluded to in Marcia Hutchinson's 'Fire Next Time', a story which takes us back even further to another significant, though lesser-known Bradford fire – the August 1981 blaze which destroyed the top

INTRODUCTION

floor of the Textile Hall, and was widely suspected to be racially motivated.

No matter where we end up, Bradfordians are tied together by the events that happen to our city. Paul in Becky Cherriman's 'The Hole in the Heart' is very real for this reason. Bradford's 'hole in the ground' was the nickname given to the stalled construction site of a large shopping and leisure complex, The Broadway. As Becky's story shows, the hole became a symbol of the turmoil we were all experiencing as individuals. As with that hole, we learn that the old must be demolished for the new to begin, and that process is challenging.

Of course, those challenges have spanned many generations of Bradford history, and inspired many a great literary work in the process. From John Braine exploring the struggles of social mobility in post-war Northern England to Andrea Dunbar's raw, unflinching accounts of life growing up on the Buttershaw estate, Bradfordian writers are synonymous for getting under the skin of their city.

The two oldest stories in this collection are particularly potent examples of this. Just a year younger than fellow Bradfordian J.B. Priestley, Malachi Whitaker has often been described as 'the Bradford Chekhov'. Her story here, 'Smoke of the Tide', demonstrates the irresistible power of place and memory. Elsewhere, Bill Broady's 'Bouncing Back' offers a Swiftian satire on an earlier, ill-fated initiative to boost tourism and investment in the city.

For good or bad, Bradford dreams differently to other places. It is out of step because it inadvertently sets the pace. The return of old-fashioned school dinner puddings and the rebirth of ice cream parlours is one example of this.

Back in the 2000s, a little way up from the Alhambra Theatre, an eatery was about to raise the bar for Bradford curry houses, when a son was handed the keys to a restaurant by his immigrant father. Fresh from university, and much to

INTRODUCTION

his father's chagrin, the dapper young man immediately upgraded the kettle for a professional coffee machine.

He had spotted a hole in the market, his customers were like him, schooled in England, with palates straddling England and Pakistan, and had nowhere to cater to their likes. He added nostalgic plates of school dinner puddings to the menu and the success was immediate.

As a reporter, I would spend evenings in the café when I was assigned the late shift. I was chasing stories and building contacts; little did I know I was developing the world that would turn into my novel, *The Khan*.

The mustard-coloured walls were covered in classic '70s Bollywood posters, the metallic tables and chairs filled with beautiful young British Asians looking for somewhere to spend their evening that didn't include alcohol – the sober movement was here long before the hipsters of 2025 discovered it – and jam roly-poly and custard was where it was at.

I still remember the speed at which pudding plates were cleared, the swirl of jam, the steam rising from the yellow custard.

Bradford contains multitudes. She is vast, and sprawling, and she cannot, and will not, be reduced to a single notion.

Bradford is duality made flesh. Industrial and post-industrial. Northern grit and global colour. History and youth, for this is one of Britain's youngest cities. Heritage collides here with possibility. Struggle sits alongside joy. Grief gives way to music. Division is wrestled into a kind of rough, generous unity.

Bradford is still dreaming. She is still shaping. She is still rising.

And to know her is to know that her story, like her people, cannot, and will not, be ignored.

Saima Mir
August 2025

The Wickedest Man in the World

David Barnett

'Mr Crowley,' simpered the man, wringing his hands as though washing them, bending low as if in the presence of a king. 'It's such an honour to receive you in Bradford.'

Mr Crowley unwound the muffler from about his bull-neck and handed it to the man, whose moustache twitched as though he had some kind of tic, while another, unseen behind him, helped him off with his greatcoat. 'It's Crowley, to rhyme with *holy*,' he said, shucking off the sleeves of his coat. 'Only my enemies say it to sound like *foully*.'

The man's hand flew to his mouth, his eyes widened, and he recommenced his wringing, this time kneading Mr Crowley's scarf. 'Careful,' said Mr Crowley mildly. 'I bought that at Cordings in The Strand.'

The man, whose name was Priestley, looked at the scarf in his hands. 'It's excellent quality, Mr Crowley. Really excellent. We rather know wool here in Bradford.'

'Hmm,' said Mr Crowley, looking around the wood-panelled entrance lobby at the top of the flight of stairs he had been led up from the street. 'For wool I care little, Mr Priestley. I would prefer to hear what you think of Thelema, in due course. First, I would very much like to investigate what you know of fine wine.'

Mr Priestley pushed the scarf into the hands of a thin man with pock-marked skin who had Mr Crowley's coat over his arm, and gestured towards the double doors. 'Then come into the temple, if you would, Mr Crowley, and let us furnish you with a suitable libation. And then we are all exceedingly keen to hear you speak.'

Priestley deferred to Mr Crowley at the doors, and he walked into the large, gas-lit room, the walls covered in murals, art nouveau depictions of sin and pleasure. A dozen men in tails and starched collars awaited him, standing in a semicircle.

'How are you finding Bradford so far, Mr Crowley?' said the boldest of them, a man of twenty or so, ten years younger than their guest, with a rakish look. At the age of 30, Mr Crowley was beginning to find youth tiresome. Vapidly dull. Even those that professed to be libertines and hedonists did so without thought. A waiter brought a tray of claret, and Mr Crowley took a glass.

'I have not seen much of Bradford, since I was collected from the station in this fog.' He sipped the wine. Sharp, tangy, cheap. He made a face.

'A right pea-souper,' agreed the young man. 'It's all the chimneys, you see. From the mills.' Mr Crowley considered him with interest. He'd seen his like many times. Ambitious. Wanted to climb the ladder in the Order. A little more outspoken than his older brethren. The man suddenly grew uncomfortable under Mr Crowley's penetrating stare, and coughed into his fist. 'Bradford is very impressive when the weather is clearer.'

'I doubt it,' said Mr Crowley. 'In the past five years I have travelled to Mexico, where I climbed Popocatepétl, and Japan, and Hong Kong, and Ceylon. I contracted malaria in Calcutta and recuperated in Rangoon. I have lived in Paris. I cannot see what delights Bradford might have to challenge the sights I have seen.'

The man leaned forward and, astonishingly, winked. 'Wait until after dinner, Mr Crowley, and we shall see.'

'That's quite plenty, Mr Greenough,' said Priestley, interjecting with a hand on Mr Crowley's arm, which he found almost as objectionable as Greenough's wink. 'Shall we sit and have dinner served?'

Mr Crowley nodded, and leaned into the young Mr Greenough. 'Inside a decade you'll be dead, sir. Riddled with bullets in the mud on some foreign field.'

Greenough blinked, and paled visibly. 'Dead, Mr Crowley? There is a war coming? The spirits have told you this? And that I–?'

'I have travelled extensively, Mr Greenough. I use my eyes, and my wit. Yes, there is a war coming. In ten years or less. Enjoy yourself while you can.'

The dinner was just about edible, overcooked lamb and undercooked potatoes, the greens all the goodness boiled out of them. With wine inside them, the members of the Bradford Number 5 Horus Temple of the Order of the Golden Dawn found their tongues, and began to excitedly ask Mr Crowley about his latest work, and when it would be published, and what he could tell them about Thelema and *The Book of the Law,* and how it had been dictated to him over three days in Egypt by a disembodied voice.

'Aiwass,' said Mr Crowley. 'The messenger of Horus himself.' He picked at the remains of his dinner, waiting for the servants to remove the plates. 'It was February of last year, in Cairo. I was honeymooning with my new wife, Rose. We spent some time in our rented rooms invoking the Egyptian deities, and messages began to come through.'

'How exciting,' said Mr Priestley, leaning forward. 'And it was this... Aiwass? He spoke directly to you?'

'At first, it was through Rose,' said Mr Crowley, warming to his subject. 'She would have periods of delirium, and told me that *they* were waiting for me. Later, she clarified this as Horus. Once, in her delirium, she took me to a museum where there was a *stele*, a wooden monument to a priest of the god Montu. Gentlemen, do you know the exhibit's number in the museum catalogue?'

They all shook their head.

'Six six six,' said Mr Crowley, sitting back in his chair as a babble of excited voices rose from around the table. From all except young Mr Greenough, ashen-faced still, and silent, pondering Mr Crowley's earlier words about the coming war.

The gentlemen forgot themselves and started a barrage of questions, to which Mr Crowley fended off with both palms raised. 'I would rather hear more about your marvellous temple, first. And then questions later.'

Mr Priestley cleared his throat and stood. 'Of course, Mr Crowley. The temple was established here on Godwin Street almost seventeen years ago, in 1888. Our chapter of the Golden Dawn had previously met in the Alexandra Hotel in Great Horton, but a dedicated temple was deemed fit as our numbers grew.'

Mr Crowley looked around the table. 'And yet now you number little more than a dozen.'

Priestley nodded sadly. 'The ongoing difficulties with the Order of the Golden Dawn, Mr Crowley…'

Mr Crowley did not need telling about that. He had more or less broken ties with the Order after all that business more than five years ago. A schism had developed between its leader, Samuel Liddell MacGregor Mathers, and the London cognoscenti. Mr Crowley had, at first, sided with Mathers, and on his orders had sought to seize the West Kensington temple and oust the rebels. The matter went to court, which found in the sitting group's favour, and Mathers and Crowley were frozen out of the Order completely. Upon his return from Egypt, Mr Crowley developed deep suspicions about Mathers, and believed he meant him ill. Just a few weeks ago, he had severed all contact with him.

Mr Crowley did not tell the Bradford assembly all this. They had reached out to him to invite him to the city, and he had been curious enough to accept, making the long journey down from Boleskine House on the shores of Loch Ness. He had half a mind to try out some of his thoughts and writings from *The Book of the Law*, which had been dictated to him in Cairo, if there was a genuine occultist or two among their number, and he also had the germ of a notion that he might use the fractured Golden Dawn groups in the provinces to build his own organisation, based around the teachings he had written down. But now he could see that the Bradford mob was nothing more than a gentlemen's club with occult trappings.

After the pudding, a doughy affair drowned in thick custard, the men all lit up cigars, and Mr Priestley announced with some trepidation that entertainment had been laid on.

'Whores,' said Mr Greenough, finding his voice – and his wink – again at last.

Mr Crowley raised an eyebrow, and Mr Priestley commenced his hand-wringing again. 'Mr Crowley...? Have we acted out of turn? They are very clean, and have been tutored in the ways of the Golden Dawn, so fully expect...' Then his hand went to his mouth again. 'Ah. You married just last year, Mr Crowley. I expect –'

'Yes, I married my dear Rose barely a year ago,' said Mr Crowley, puffing deep on his cigar. 'And she is with child. I think I would like to take a little stroll around the town, walk off that excellent dinner.'

Mr Priestley looked crestfallen as Mr Crowley stood and beckoned for his coat. 'We have indeed acted out of turn. My apologies. I shall send the women away.'

'Oh, don't do that, Priestley. We shall enjoy them on my return.' Finally, Mr Crowley gifted Mr Priestley the smile he was so desperate to receive. 'For am I not, as the newspapers proclaim, the Wickedest Man in the World?'

Lili had run away. Again. She would go home, of course. Everyone knew it; her mum knew it, Wayne knew it, and she knew it. She had nowhere else to go. And she wasn't dressed for running away. Skirt too short, top too skimpy, heels too high. *You're not going out dressed like that,* Wayne had proclaimed. *You're not my dad,* Lili had responded immediately. One time, it would have taken several steps to get from one to the other, demands and insults thrown while her mum sat in the chair and watched silently from one to the other and back again, as though spectating at tennis. Now Lili cut straight to the chase. Well, he wasn't her dad. And she was going out like that. And for good. They'd never see her again. Though, of course, they would.

The fog had enveloped Bradford city centre, her bus driving into a bank of it from at one moment clear streets, and then thick grey, which car headlights barely penetrated. 'Was this forecast?' somebody on the bus said. 'I'm sure this wasn't forecast.'

One day Lili *would* run away, she thought as she stood, teeth chattering, on Godwin Street. One day she'd scrape together enough money to buy a train ticket to London, or a plane ticket to Ibiza, and then she'd go. Never look back. With a pang to her shivering chest, she thought about the raised voices she'd heard as she slammed the front door behind her. Wayne was in a fury. No doubt her mum would have had a good hiding by now.

The streetlights looked like cottony pale moons in the fog. Lili could barely see her hand in front of her face. As she'd gone out anyway she could have met Asif as she was planning to, but she really couldn't be bothered with him. With anyone. She just wanted to be alone. She said the words out loud, in a thick foreign accent, like she'd seen in an old film once. 'I vant to be alone.'

Then, suddenly, she wasn't. A broad black shape loomed out of the fog towards her, crossing the road, though she couldn't actually be sure where the pavement ended and the road began. Her heart skipped, and not in a good way, but she stood her ground and straightened herself up to her full five-foot-four. That was one thing her dad had taught her before he died. *Always stand your ground, Lili. Always look 'em in the eye and show no fear.*

She wished her dad were here now. The figure moved towards her, then stopped. A man, wrapped in a thick black coat, a hat on his head. A big bear of a man, carrying a cane, which he leaned on while he looked at her, his eyes piercing and unblinking. His gaze fell to her feet and travelled the length of her to her cheap hair extensions, and finally settled on her own eyes.

'Are you a whore?' The voice a rich rumble, not a Bradford accent. She couldn't place it at all.

'Cheeky twat,' said Lili. 'Are you a nonce?' She kept her voice steady, but she was scared. He was a big man, and this fog... it made it feel like they were the only two people in the city centre. In the world.

The man's eyes narrowed. 'Nonce?' He seemed to be trying the word out for the first time.

'Yeah. Paedo. Wrong 'un. Nonce. I'm only fifteen, you know. I'm waiting for my dad. He'll be here in a minute.'

The man looked up and down Godwin Street, but the fog was thicker than ever. His brow furrowed, and he took off his hat. He was completely bald. He seemed confused. Lili wondered if he was a mental patient, or had dementia, like her nan had before she died. She said, 'Are you all right, mate? Are you lost?'

The man rubbed his chin. 'This place seems... the smell of it. The sound of it. It seems different. The air tastes...' He shook his head and looked back at Lili. 'I forget my manners. My name is Crowley. Aleister Crowley. I am visiting some gentlemen up yonder. I stepped out for a bit of air after dinner and before... the entertainment.'

Lili looked away, feigning nonchalance, though there was something about the man, something about his presence, his size, his weirdness, that made her want to stare at him. 'Yeah, all right, I don't need your life story.'

'I apologise for my earlier comment,' said the man, Aleister. 'I think I can surmise what you mean by *nonce*, and I assure you I mean you no harm.'

'Fine, we're good then,' said Lili, tapping her foot on the pavement. 'My dad'll be here soon.'

'Yes, you said.' Aleister took out of his inside coat pocket a small metal square, and popped it open to reveal a line of cigarettes. 'Do you indulge?'

Lili plucked one out and sniffed it. 'These aren't Rothmans Superkings.'

'A blend put together for me by the House of Carreras,' said Aleister. He took one and struck a match, puffing it into life, then held the match to her, cupped in his hand. Lili hesitated. There could be anything in these cigs. He could be trying to spike her. But she'd taken a random one, and so had Aleister, so she allowed him to bring the match closer until the end of her cigarette ignited.

Lili took a long drag. It was better than the fags her mum bought which she nicked occasionally. She looked at Aleister, leaning on his cane, smoking thoughtfully. 'So how was your gentlemen's club thing? Why are you here?'

'Tiresome,' said Aleister. 'I'm here to talk about my book, which we haven't even got round to yet.'

'Are you an author?' said Lili, suddenly interested. Her English teacher said she was good at writing stories. She enjoyed it. She nicked books from Waterstones all the time. Well, it wasn't her fault they'd closed down the library near her. 'What's your book about?'

Aleister looked at her for a long moment. 'You have me at a disadvantage.'

'What does that mean?'

'I don't know your name.'

Lili said, 'Oh, right. It's Lili. With two I's.'

'Of course you have two eyes,' said Aleister, a smile on his fleshy lips. 'Quite arresting ones of the deepest brown.'

Lili laughed despite herself. 'You know what I mean. It's spelled with two I's. L-I-L-I. It's short for Lilith, actually. My dad named me. He's dead.' She looked away, conscious she was talking too much.

'Was your father a practitioner of magick?' said Aleister.

'Because he called me Lilith and it's a bit witchy?'

'That, and you said he is meeting you here. Which is quite an achievement for a dead man.'

There was a time, when Lili was very young, that she believed her dad could do anything. Even come back from the dead. But when the cancer took him, and he withered and shrank before her eyes, she knew she'd been wrong. He was just like everyone else. He got ill and died. There was nothing special about him at all. If there was, he wouldn't have gone away, would he? And let Mum hook up with bastard Wayne, and make all their lives a misery.

'So, your book,' Lili said, to change the subject. 'What's it about?'

How to explain the teachings of Aiwass to a child? Relay the word of a god to a mere girl? And why was he even bothering? Mr Crowley plucked his fob watch from his pocket, but it seemed to have stopped. He held it to his ear and put it away. He should be getting back to the temple. But something about this girl, her manner and her bearing, fascinated him. She seemed like no child he had met before.

Mr Crowley said, 'It is to be called *The Book of the Law*.'

The girl sniffed somewhat derisory. 'Sounds boring. Are you a solicitor or something, then?'

'No, I myself am a practitioner of magick,' said Mr Crowley. 'A libertarian in thought and deed. It is not about the law of the land, but the only law. It was dictated to me—'

'TL;DR,' said Lili.

Mr Crowley stared at her. 'What?'

'Just the headlines, please.' She shivered in the cold fog that enveloped them.

Mr Crowley suppressed a smile. 'Very well, there is but one law, and this is the whole of it: Do as thou wilt.'

The girl spread her palms and shook her head. 'Meaning?'

Mr Crowley took a deep breath. 'Meaning, every single one among us should do precisely what they please. And that is that.'

Lili nudged with the toe of her high-heeled shoe a broken brick, lying against the stone wall of the building that reared up beside them, and stared down at it. 'So everybody should just do what they want, whatever it is, whenever they feel like it?'

'Precisely.'

'Like, if I wanted to pick up that brick and throw it through the window of this shop, I should just do it?'

'If that would please you, yes.'

She bent down and picked up the brick, weighing it in her hand. Mr Crowley glanced at the window of the shop, and frowned. The words on the gaudy signs made no sense to him. The wares in the window were... what, exactly?

'What manner of store is this?' he said.

'Vape shop,' said Lili. 'Should I do it?'

Mr Crowley turned back to her. 'Do not ask me. Ask yourself. If it be thy will, then proceed.'

Lili took a step back, to where the kerb probably was, hidden in the mist, and faced the window, hefting the brick like she was about to putt the shot. Mr Crowley said, 'Why do you wish to do this?'

'Because I hate everybody,' answered Lili fiercely and without hesitation. 'I hate Wayne for being a twat and I hate Mum for letting him get away with it and I hate Dad for dying and I hate school and I hate my stupid Saturday job at the shop and I hate my boyfriend and I hate everybody and everything.'

Mr Crowley shrugged. 'Valid enough reasons.'

Then with a strength belying her thin frame, and a scream ripped from Hell itself, Lili launched the brick at the window of the shop. It connected and the glass shattered, exploding inwards, the crash echoing around the tall buildings, then swallowed by the fog. Mr Crowley was about to say something when suddenly there was the most piercing sound that assaulted his ears, a high-pitched tonal shrieking.

Lili's eyes widened and she covered her mouth with her hands. 'Shit. An alarm. We should get out of here before the feds arrive.'

Then she was off, running down the hill, almost disappearing into the fog. Mr Crowley hurried after her. 'Feds?'

'Police,' she called over her shoulder. She was laughing, somewhat maniacally. 'Shit. I can't believe I did that.'

No, it would not do to be arrested by the constabulary in the presence of this strange girl, decided Mr Crowley, and picked up the pace as best he could, following the indistinct shape of Lili in the fog ahead of him. He did not want to get too far from the temple; if he lost his way in this weather he doubted he would find his way back. But Lili had stopped ahead of him, and he huffed up to her, leaning on his cane to catch his breath.

The fog seemed infused with multicoloured lights all around, and he could hear the sound of flowing water, but could see nothing more. 'Where are we?'

'City Park,' said Lili. She buried her face in her hands and said again, 'I can't believe I did that.'

'Do you feel better?' said Mr Crowley, squinting at her. She would be the first ordinary soul to put the teachings of Horus into actual practice, and he was curious as to how she felt. This could make an addendum for *The Book of the Law*.

Lili looked at him. 'No. I feel fucking terrible.'

'Why?' asked Mr Crowley with curiosity. 'It was what you wanted to do, more than anything. So you did it. Do you not feel free? Liberated?'

'I smashed the window of a shop,' said Lili. 'It was wrong.'

'According to the strictures of society.'

'No, according to me.' She stared at him. 'People can't just go around doing what they want all the time. Not when it hurts other people.'

'Tell me more,' said Mr Crowley, leaning on his cane again. He was interested in her moral reasoning here. 'What care you for others? You said yourself, you hate everyone. Your school. Your employment. Your own family.'

Lili stared at her feet. 'I don't, not really. Not proper hate. Well, apart from Wayne, obviously.' Then she looked back at him. 'If everybody did what they wanted and got away with it, it would be the people like Wayne who get on, wouldn't it? The bullies. The nutjobs. Bad people. Your stupid law only helps bad people do what they want and get away with it. People like my mum, and me, and ordinary people, they'd just get the crappy end of the stick.'

Mr Crowley considered. 'You think the law of Horus is inequitable? It is weighted towards the strong? The privileged? The unscrupulous?'

'Everything is, all the time,' said Lili. She looked Mr Crowley up and down. 'You'd never get it. You look like you're rich. Fancy clothes. Gentlemen's clubs. Yeah, it'd be fine for you, a rich white man, to do what he wants all the time. It'd be people like me who got shat on.'

'Shat on,' mused Mr Crowley. The girl's provincial language was colourful and her meaning not always clear to him, but he was finding her summation interesting. Far more than that of the hangers-on who declared every word he uttered to be some small work of genius.

'Yeah. I mean, people have to look out for each other, don't they?'

Mr Crowley gazed into the fog. 'In Paris I read the works of Pierre Leroux, who contested that individualism was wrong, that people did not exist in isolation of each other. I found this idea of *socialism* to be infantile and unworkable. And yet…'

'I was only ten when my dad died,' said Lili quietly. 'My mum had a breakdown. I didn't know what that meant at the time. She just couldn't get out of bed. She couldn't get shopping in. Wash my clothes. I missed school. After a few days the neighbours came round. They cooked meals and did the laundry. One of them took me to school every day and another picked me up.' She looked at Mr Crowley. 'I'm sure none of them actually *wanted* to do that, not really. They probably had better things to do and money was tight for them as well. But they did it.'

Mr Crowley gazed into the light-infused fog for a while, and momentarily the writhing mist began to clear, revealing a large billboard or some-such. He read the words aloud. 'Bradford. UK City of Culture. But what do those numbers mean?'

Lili squinted into the fog, and laughed. 'Twenty twenty-five. That's the year.'

Mr Crowley looked at her. 'The year?'

'This year. Twenty twenty-five. City of Culture year. In Bradford.' She frowned. 'Are you all right?'

He knew he had paled somewhat, felt the blood draining from his face, and leaned heavily on his cane. 'Some joke? Or prank? Two thousand and twenty-five?'

Lili laughed again. 'What year do you think it is?'

'Nineteen-hundred and five, which I do not *think*, but I *know*,' said Mr Crowley with some effort, his mouth dry. He swallowed as best he could and said, 'You seek to jape me, Lili.'

She shrugged and looked away. 'Whatever.'

Mr Crowley gripped her arm. 'Are you claiming you speak the truth? That I have… somehow been plunged into a vision of the future? Like Faust? One hundred and twenty years hence? Tell me! Tell me the truth!'

'Get off me!' shouted Lili, tearing her arm out of his grip. 'You *are* a fucking nonce! I knew it!'

Mr Crowley stepped back, his hand raised in supplication. 'I apologise. This is quite a lot to take in. I regret seizing you in this manner. Perhaps I am, as the newspapers claim, the Wickedest Man in the World after all.'

Lili rubbed her arm, glaring at him, then looked away. 'You reckon so? You haven't met Wayne.'

Mr Crowley took a second to compose himself, his mind spinning like a dervish. 'Tell me about this Wayne,' he said, by way of calming the turmoil within him.

What was there to say about bastard Wayne? Mum had hooked up with him three years ago. He started hitting her six months later. And the few times Lili had tried to intervene, she got the business end of his fists as well. These days, when the rows started, she locked herself in her room and buried her face in her pillow, listening to Spotify at full volume.

'He does nothing,' said Lili. 'Never worked a day in his life. Just drinks and smokes his Universal Credit and shares stupid Facebook memes about immigrants and vaccines. God, I hate him.' She felt the anger rising in her again. Wanted to smash another window.

'I understand barely half of what you say,' said Aleister quietly. 'He hates foreigners?'

Lili nodded. 'Last year he got a train to Sheffield and tried to set fire to a hotel with asylum seekers in it. All the trouble last summer? God, I prayed he'd get banged up but the lucky bastard didn't get caught.'

'So why don't you leave?'

Lili looked down at herself, her legs blue and mottled with cold. 'I have, sort of. Run away. But I'll have to go back. I can't leave my mum with him, Aleister. I can't leave her on her own.'

'Hmmm.' Aleister seemed to consider for a moment, then dug into his pocket and produced a shiny coin. 'This farthing is cursed.'

Lili took it from him and inspected it. It was an old coin, it had a picture of an old bald man on one side and on the other, Britannia. She knew who that was. Wayne had a tattoo of her on his leg. Above Britannia it said FARTHING and below, 1905. She said, 'What do you mean, cursed?'

'I cursed it myself, with dark magick. It's a simple matter to do so. It's yours. Slip it into his pocket, and think what you might want to happen to him. He could fall under a carriage, or have a heart attack, or choke on his porridge.'

'As easy as that, huh?'

Aleister fixed her with his piercing gaze. 'Magick is real, Lili.'

She opened her little handbag and dropped it in with the other coins, hesitating a moment before closing it. 'Maybe it could make him a better man to my mum.'

Aleister barked a laugh. 'Making a bad man into a good one is not a punishment.'

'Maybe it is if you're wicked,' said Lili. 'Maybe it's the worst sort of punishment. Anyway, I won't do that. Being good only matters if it's your decision, not if you're forced into it. I'll think about it.' She looked at Aleister. 'So, what happens now?'

He looked reflectively into the fog. 'Perhaps I could stay here, in the world of twenty twenty-five. What marvels and wonders must there be?' Suddenly he looked off, towards the main road. 'Did you hear that? I could have sworn...'

'I didn't hear anything,' said Lili. 'So you have nothing to go back to? In Nineteen-oh-five?'

'I have a wife, who is about to have a baby,' said Aleister thoughtfully. 'And I must make efforts to publish my book. There is also the matter of the instructions handed down to me from Horus.'

'Instructions?'

Aleister began to count off on his fingers. 'I am meant to procure, by which means I know not, an ancient artefact from a museum in Egypt, which has the exhibit number 666. I am supposed to translate *The Book of the Law* into every language in the world. I am to find an island to live on, and fortify it.'

'Your own book says you have to do all those things? That sounds like a lot of work,' said Lili. 'I thought there was only meant to be one law? Do as thou wilt.'

'Yes,' said Aleister thoughtfully. 'That is a very good point.' He whirled around again. 'Did you not hear that? Someone calling my name.'

'I didn't hear anything,' said Lili. 'Look, I'd better get to the bus stop. God knows what Wayne's been up to while I've been gone. I need to check on my mum. Hope you get home OK, Aleister. It was… interesting.'

The voice sounded closer now, surely just feet away, calling his name. Mr Crowley turned and peered into the fog as a dim shape appeared, and then coalesced into the young Mr Greenough.

'Mr Crowley! Thank God! We thought you must have become lost in this damnable fog. We've been looking for you.'

'I'm fine, Mr Greenough,' said Mr Crowley. He felt relief – and, it had to be said, disappointment – welling within him. If Mr Greenough was here, then it was indeed a jape, a prank, that this was somehow one hundred and twenty years hence. 'I have been having a most interesting conversation with–'

Mr Crowley turned, but Lili had gone. And the coloured lights that had suffused the fog… they had gone, also. Only the dim lights of gas lamps filtered through. The big billboard was no longer to be seen. 'Lili?' he called, but there was no answer. Wherever he had stood a moment ago, he was no longer there, the stone was different underfoot. The air smelled thickly of coke. Had Lili been a ghost from the future? Or had he, for a short while, been a ghost from the past?

'Let's get you back to the temple, Mr Crowley,' said Mr Greenough.

After warming himself by the fire and with copious amounts of brandy, Mr Crowley took to the small lectern that had been set up in front of the small assembly in the temple. Mr Priestley had said, 'Whores first, or discussion, Mr Crowley?'

In truth, his heart was set on neither, but he opted first to talk about *The Book of the Law* and its teachings. He retrieved his manuscript from his leather bag and stood at the lectern, gathering his thoughts, staring at the typewritten papers.

There is but one law, and this is the whole of it: Do as thou wilt, he had said to Lili.

Your own book says you have to do all those things? That sounds like a lot of work, she had said back.

Mr Crowley cleared his throat. 'Over three days this manuscript was dictated to me. It is the word of Horus and it heralds a new Aeon. A new era, where there is only one law. Do as thou wilt.'

The gentlemen applauded. Mr Crowley held up his hand. 'And yet... and yet, it demands so much of me.' He leaned on the lectern, inspecting the men in front of him. 'And truly, can everyone really do as they will? Can all men act without consequence? Without another man suffering?'

Mr Greenough raised his hand. 'Mr Crowley? Are you... are you doubting the word of Horus?'

Mr Crowley glared at him, and swallowed drily. What *was* he saying? Why was he talking like this? He shoved his hand into his pocket for his flask of good brandy, not the stuff they were serving him here, and his fingers closed around a coin. It felt thick and heavy, and he fished it out, and inspected it in the gaslight. It had a curious shape and weight, silver with a gold outer rim. On one side was an engraving of two bees, on the other an aquiline profile. It said 2023 CHARLES III.

Lili must have slipped it into his pocket. It was quite a

simple matter to curse a coin with magick, he'd said so himself. Mr Crowley laughed. Then he gathered up the pages of his book, turned and walked calmly to the fire, and threw them into the flames.

There was a tumult of voices, and Mr Crowley raised his hand. 'I am sorry to cut this evening short, gentlemen, but I appear to have been cursed while out in the fog. I wish to return to my hotel and take the first train to Scotland in the morning, where I will spend some time with my wife and unborn child.' He mused for a moment while his coat was fetched, and said, 'If it is a girl, I think I shall persuade Rose to call her Lilith.'

Mr Priestley hovered around in front of him. 'Cursed, Mr Crowley? Cursed? Here in Bradford? Whatever do you mean? And your book… the fire…'

'Oh, there are many other copies squirrelled away in Boleskine House. No doubt I shall revisit it when the mood takes me. For now, I must abide by the terms of the curse.' Mr Crowley held up the coin, and flipped it with his thumb, watching it spin in the air. He held out his palm to catch it, but between reaching its zenith and beginning to fall, it simply disappeared.

'But a *curse*, Mr Crowley?' said Mr Priestley, commencing his anguished hand-wringing.

'The very worst for the Wickedest Man in the World,' said Mr Crowley with a smile. 'I am to be a good person. At least, for a short while.'

In his coat and with his muffler wrapped around his neck, Mr Crowley followed Mr Priestley down the stairs to Godwin Street. The fog had dissipated, the night was clear, the stars winking above. Soot-stained but mighty, Bradford suddenly did seem, to Mr Crowley's eyes, to be as enticing and as filled with mystery as Paris or Rangoon or Cairo. The Wickedest Man in the World tipped his homburg hat at the confusion of gathering gentlemen, and set off for the Midland Hotel, to ponder, and then to sleep, and then to go home.

Smoke of the Tide

Malachi Whitaker

A FAIR, MIDDLE-AGED MAN with a red face and prominent, light-blue eyes, walked out of the door of a pleasant-looking cottage in the High Street. Dusk was deepening into night as he left, and a few stars showed in the sky directly above him. They looked pale because of a steady red glow that came from the village fairground. Over the cottage roofs that stood between him and the fair, strong, black smoke rolled, taking the gleam from the light beneath it. He drew up the smell into his nostrils, and quivered as a certain rapture took hold of him.

The name of the man was Albert Shepherd. He had been born in the cottage which he had just left; indeed, his father and mother still lived there, although all their children had married and left them. Albert was the youngest, and he had been the most successful; that is to say, in northern standards, he had made a lot of brass. He was married to a London woman, and did not often come home, because she could not see the astonishing beauty of the industrial north; she thought it was dirty and depressing. The blue-grey landscapes with their design of mill chimneys – Marion called them smokestacks, and nobody knew what she meant – the rolling hills, the mingling of smoke and cloud, the white steam from the dye-houses, the cobbled streets and houses of blackened stone; all this meant nothing to Marion.

It meant a great deal to Albert Shepherd. He was never fully happy in the south. He loved his wife, and lived there because she liked it best. However, every now and then his homesickness would be too much for him, and he would suddenly say, 'I have to go to Bradford on business.' Each time he asked her to go with him, and each time she refused.

He had not been home in September for years. When he had arrived yesterday there had been a great commotion on the Green. Steam wagons were clanking and snorting, and caravans were springing up like mushrooms across the road from the spare ground. Children were running about shrieking, 'The Tide – the Tide's come!'

It was twenty years since he had smelt the smoke of the Tide. Here, a fair was called either a Feast or a Tide; mostly the latter. He recalled how often he, and the other boys in the school close by, had heard the measured hammering as the Tide was being set up, and how they had longed for the morning to go and the evening to come so that they could rush in and see everything, and spend their money. Even when the money was spent there were other things to watch; other people spending theirs, sometimes winning, more often losing, at games of chance.

This Saturday night, twenty years after, he wanted just as badly to go again. For some whim, he had put only one and sixpence in his pocket. He remembered thinking, when he was ten, that one and sixpence would have been the ideal sum to take to the Tide. When he had had only threepence it had seemed that the very fruits of paradise could have been got for one and six. Well, he would see.

He hastened his footsteps to get there, rattling his coppers in his fingers, and whistling the tune that, out of three, came loudest to his ears through the air.

Raucous shouts, laughter, raised voices, blaring music, the occasional ring of a bell as some champion mallet-slinger touched the tam-o'-shanter of Donald Dinnie, met him as he entered the stall-lined avenue. Here were children's toys, balloons, and brandy snap. Always he had wanted to buy some brandy snap, but his mother would never let him have any. Instead, she made her own, and sometimes, if she left it a second too long in the oven, it was burnt a deep brown, instead of being the pale yellow of his dreams. At last he would have some. As other people were waiting before him he saw the price. 'Nay,' he thought, 'if I spend fourpence of my one and six I shan't have much left.' Casting a lingering glance at the yellow brandy snap, he moved away.

There was so much to see! At one sideshow there were some balls which had merely to be rolled into holes. It looked easy. The amount of the prize was written above each hole, threepence, sixpence – on one, a shilling.

He bought three balls for threepence and rolled them carefully down. The very first one stopped in the shilling place, the second missed, and the third fell into the three-penny hole. He shouted 'Sithar' as pleased as a child and, instead of trying again, he picked up his winnings and walked away, leaving a crowd behind him, gazing and exclaiming after him. He heard a voice saying, 'It's Albert Shepherd, wheer's 'e sprung from?'

He looked about, trying to place the voice, but the seething crowd prevented him from finding out what he wanted to know. Somebody else would be sure to recognise him. He longed wistfully for a friend, one with whom he could share his happiness. He looked up at the hundred waving legs which were rushing through the air not far above him in the Flying Chairs. Each time the machine gyrated, the flying chairs and flying legs came nearer to his head. He wondered whether he dare risk these, and decided not to.

'I'll have six goes on the motor cars with my winnings,' he told himself.

How delightful it was in the motor cars, better by far than in his own. These were upholstered in red plush; they went down a valley, up a hill, down a valley, up a hill with great speed and regularity. He couldn't help saying 'Whoo-hoo' each time the motorcar he was in arrived at the exact middle of the dip.

From the centrepiece, inside which a greasy-looking man counted piles of coppers, came the loud, intoxicating blare of a popular song. The second time it was played he hummed it. A little painted image of a man, with a feather in his hat, tapped at a drum, and at each tap a great drum beat from somewhere inside. It was entrancing to meet, on one side, this little iron man, who stared so bravely before him, and tapped away so obediently; yet it was just as entrancing to roll around to the other side, where the real man kept on counting his piles of coppers.

Round and round he went. The faces of all the people in the fairground below were bathed in floods of light. From here he could see little boys darting among the crowd, looking for stray dropped pennies. Albert Shepherd couldn't help laughing to himself. He seemed to be riding above the cares of all the world. There was no time to think of care; always a hill or a valley loomed ahead, and a mad noise urged you on. Away with the dull streets, the hidden offices, the slights and drawbacks even successful men have to meet in business!

Suddenly he thought, 'If only Marion had liked this. If only I had gone to work at the mill every day, like father, and Marion had been happy and contented, like mother. Once a year we could have brought the kids down to the Tide – poor little devils, Marion never lets 'em get within miles of one – and bought 'em a red and yellow wheelbarrow apiece.'

His face clouded over with sadness, to think that they would never know this joy. 'What's in front of them?' he thought; 'the way Marion's bringin' 'em up, they'll soon grow ashamed of her and me.' He made a sudden resolution. He would send for the children in spite of Marion's protests, and let them spend the day with their granny. On Monday night he would take them to the Tide. What did it matter if their bedtime was early, they should stay up until ten for once. Let them get hold of this before their cage claimed them; let them have something bright to look back on. What did it matter if it was tawdry? Everybody needs a bit of tinsel once in a few years.

When he had had four rides, he got up and walked unsteadily down the wooden platform. As he went, he nodded to the little man with the drum.

After the excitement of the cars, it seemed quieter down among the people. Some stopped him and spoke; old men tottering in with their children and grandchildren greeted him and treated him like a boy. 'Nah then, Albert, what's tha' doin' 'ere bi thysel'?'

Over in one corner he met the blacksmith, on whom he had played a number of boyish tricks. He always felt a little ashamed in front of this man. The smith was throwing wooden balls at coconuts, as yet without success. They began to talk together. Some young lads brushed past them, chased by a crowd of shrieking girls with feather dusters in their hands and imitation beetles on the end of tiny wooden ladders.

The blacksmith spat in disgust.

'Lads aren't what they used to be,' he said. 'Now when I wa' smithyin' down at quarry, thirty year sin, lads wor lads. Ther' was one young devil 'at used to play a trick on me ivery morn. 'E used to climb up to t'chimbley, an' put a slate across t'top, an' as sooin as Ah fired up, place filled wi' smoke. Ah niver could remember, an' Ah niver catched 'im, but they don't do things like that now. They daresn't. They run away from lasses i'stead.'

Albert Shepherd looked up at this bulky old man who towered above him and laughed inwardly. It was he who used to climb up and put the slate over the chimney to smoke the blacksmith out, but he did not dare to say so. He bought some wooden balls and began aimlessly throwing them at a young man who was trotting up and down behind a high netting with three hats piled on his head. You had to knock the top one off. He found he could knock off the hat, or all three hats, quite easily, and did it so many times that the man asked him humbly to stop it. 'I'm not the right chap,' he said, 'and I'm not used to this. The right chap's got a less 'ead than me, and the 'ats fit 'im tighter.'

Excited by his victories, Albert offered to change places with him, and the man came out grinning and rubbing his neck. Soon a crowd drew round, and money poured in. Albert found it hard to walk backwards and forwards in an unconcerned way. As soon as he saw a ball coming, he would flinch and duck, so that his hats were rarely knocked off. He was forced to smile as he wondered what Marion or his business friends would think if they saw him running up and down inside a netting at a fair, having his hat knocked off.

The music from the motor cars, the flying chairs and the roundabouts came all together into his ears. When one tune stopped, and only two strove for mastery, his spirits lowered; as soon as the third tune got up again they returned. All at once, he saw his father and mother. He laughed, and turned away his face, but to no purpose. Through all the din his mother's voice broke accusingly, 'Our Albert, come out!' and he obeyed it, as he had obeyed it a hundred times before, in his younger days.

He went with them to the sideshows, the dartboard and the ringboard; many a game he won. He got boxes of toffee, and egg cups, and china mugs, and strange little ornaments, the kind his mother loved to put on her bedroom mantelpiece. He did not remember when he had last felt so happy.

Each year his mother and father came down to the Tide, just for a walk round, to see old friends; very soon they went back home. This night their son did not go with them. It grew later and later and, one by one, the stalls were shut down. For the last time the harsh music crashed out, and above it you could hear the steady thump, thump of the Tide's heart – the great power engine which drove the roundabouts.

Instead of going home, Albert Shepherd went for a short walk, up a green lane on the hillside. In his pockets a number of pennies still rattled – so far as he had counted he had elevenpence left – and in his nostrils the smell of the thick smoke lingered.

He met a policeman, walking with slow, even steps.

'Good night,' he said; he could see it was Willie Ambler, a boy who had been at school with him.

'Hello, Albert,' said the policeman, 'how long are you over for? Did you come just for t'feeast, like?'

'Ay,' answered Albert, 'I've just had a look in at t'Tide.' Marion hated to hear him talk like this, he reflected.

'It gets worse ivery year, doesn't it?' said the policeman, gazing yearningly over at the spot where the smoke still rolled up to the exquisite midnight sky, in which a full round moon was now sailing.

'Ay,' said Albert. It would never do for them both to confess how deeply they loved it; so they stood there for a long time, until the glow died away, and only the moon was left serenely looking down.

Samosas and Parkin

Abda Khan

'You want to wring them out a bit more, love!' she said, in her thick Yorkshire accent.

That was the first time I saw and heard her, on that chilly October morning in 1972, a few days after I had arrived at my new home in this place called Bradford which was pronounced more like 'Brrat-fud'. I was in the small yard of our rear back-to-back terraced house, absent-mindedly tossing the clothes that I had just washed by hand at the kitchen sink, onto the clothes line. She and her husband lived next door; our properties parted by the path which led off from the shared tunnel giving access to our houses and the outdoor toilets at the very end.

She shoved the bag of rubbish she was carrying into the large tin can bin with the rusty lid that sat by the stone wall at the back of her yard, after which she marched over towards me.

'Let me give you a hand,' she said, in her unique dulcet tones that I would come to know as a derivative of the thick Yorkshire accent – the Bradfordian twang. She pulled out one of my kameez's from the pile of soaking clothes and started to twist and turn it, leaving a puddle underneath that drifted away through the cracks in the ground and towards the dip in the path.

'My name's Anna,' she said, as she held out her right hand.

I thought she was the prettiest woman I had ever seen, with her shoulder-length brown hair and hazel eyes, wearing a fashionable checked brown skirt and camel-coloured thick belted jumper that hugged her slim waist. She would later tell me that she had thought that I was the prettiest woman she had ever seen with my golden skin, high cheekbones, jet black hair and soft brown eyes.

'My name is Reshma,' I replied, as my brown hand met her white one.

'Oh good, you speak English,' she said with a smile.

'Not very good, but okay I think,' I responded.

'Well, that'll do!' she said, and we both quietly got on with properly squeezing the rest of the clothes and pegging them on to the line.

New to Bradford, a cold and foggy place that seemed like a million miles from my life in a sleepy but sunny little village in Pakistan, I did not have the first clue about the neighbourhood I found myself in, so Anna took it upon herself to show me around the Barkerend area. We trundled and chatted as we went from the best grocers shop for the freshest Mothers Pride bread and the tastiest fruit and veg, to the post office where I would purchase and post my blue 'par avion' letters to keep in contact with my beloved family back home, and of course the local fish and chip shop for which I would save my pennies so I could occasionally go with her to buy a chippy lunch with extra salt and vinegar all neatly parcelled up in yesterday's edition of the *Telegraph & Argus*.

Anna would drop her son Peter, who had recently turned five years old, to Barkerend Primary school every morning for quarter to nine and pick him up at half past three in the afternoon. Sometimes, I would tag along as well, and we would run to the shops together for the groceries we needed for the next day or two. Unlike our husbands, neither of us worked, although coincidentally both our husbands worked at the same place, her other half a supervisor, and mine a manual labourer, at one of the largest local employers, Barkerend Mills, famous for the worsted wool from which were made the finest wool suits.

Quite often, we would end up having afternoon tea together, and Anna surprised herself when she realised she actually loved spicy food, as well as my milky masala chai which we alternated with the regular English tea. My freshly fried golden crispy samosas soon became a staple at our little tea parties. 'These spicy pastry things are going to be the next big thing, mark my words' she'd say, followed by 'you need to start selling these, you'll definitely make a bob or two.' But I'd often threaten her that I would only show up with my samosas if she promised to make her gingery Yorkshire Parkin. Sometimes she would ring the changes, and make sweet sticky strawberry jam tarts, or a Victoria sponge fit for a queen, or jammy coconut squares, but my personal favourite was always the spiced treacly ginger cake.

My husband and I didn't yet have a television, and I remember being so excited initially to be able to watch the small black and white TV at Anna's house, but as we would meet in the daytime when our husbands were at work, there only ever seemed to be educational shows for schools and colleges on at that time, so that excitement soon fizzled out. We preferred to have music on in the background instead. Sundays were different though. Until we bought our first, very second hand, television a few years later, every Sunday morning, at 9am sharp, I would turn up next door (sometimes accompanied by my husband, sometimes without him) to watch the only programme I properly understood and thoroughly enjoyed, and the only programme Anna (and her husband if he was there) would sit and watch cluelessly. *Nayi Zindagi Naya Jeevan* on BBC2 was my happy place. As soon as that introduction played, my excitement heightened, and for the next blissful 30 minutes the rest of the world stood still as I was royally entertained with all things South Asian – news from the region, exciting interviews with desi film stars, live performances from the top singers from back home. The melodies that swayed into the room for those 30 minutes reminded me of the warm breeze that I used to feel when running carelessly, barefoot, through the corn fields, or eagerly flying kites on the rooftop terrace, or sitting in the courtyard under the shade of the peepal tree eating fresh buffalo ghee parathas with thick creamy homemade yogurt and mum's tangy mango and lime pickle, washing it all down with sweetly spiced milky tea. For that half an hour, I felt the sun on my face, and had this warm fuzzy feeling inside that no one could spoil. For those 30 minutes, I really would forget how cold and dark life was in this country.

On a particularly cold December day the following year, we sat by the coal fire I had lit in my living room, soaking in the heat from the flames, sharing our samosas and ginger cake, and sipping hot cinnamon and cardamom tea.

'You remember I told you my husband has a very important work dinner coming up tomorrow evening,' Anna reminded me.

'Yes, I remember,' I said, as I grabbed the steel poker and jabbed the fire, moving the coal around in an attempt to rustle up some extra heat.

'Well, I have been invited to go along too. And between you and me, I think he might be due a promotion!'

'How exciting!'

'And another thing,' said Anna, as she reached for her second samosa and a spoonful of mint chutney, 'you won't believe where the dinner is! It's only at the Norfolk Gardens Hotel! My husband told me this morning.'

'Wow! That brand new hotel in town, near the town hall!' I could only dream of being invited to such a modern hotel.

My husband was a simple machine operative, there was never going to be any such invite for us. Hotels like that were where posh people went, or white people, or both. 'What are you going to wear? Perhaps that lovely dark green dress you showed me once?' I asked her, coming back to the present conversation.

'Yes, the very one, seeing as though it is the only thing I have that is nice enough. I bought it in the sales last year from Brown Muffs, it was such a good price, I couldn't resist. I have been saving it for a special occasion. There are going to be lots of senior managers there, and the factory owners, and all their wives, and I am sure they will all have their finest clothes on, so I don't want to look out of place.'

'You will look beautiful, my friend,' I told her.

'I hope so. I know this dinner means a great deal to my husband – I think there is a lot riding on how it goes. You could say it is sort of part of the interview process. I suppose they want to see him mingle with the big wigs, and be sure that he is ready to join the heady echelons of top management.'

'Ech-e-lons?' I asked.

'Ah, yes, well, that means a high position or rank,' Anna explained.

I thought about that word after she left for quite some time. 'Echelons'. Whilst our respective husbands worked at the same place, my husband was at the very bottom and on the lowest wage of all the people that worked at that mill. I wondered what the word was for that – what the opposite of 'echelons' was. It was so hard making ends meet, and with the pressure to send money back home to his aging parents, we were left with next to nothing once all the bills were paid. I was still excited for Anna and her husband though – he worked hard and deserved to be rewarded for it. And I loved to see how excited Anna was about this dinner.

You can imagine my surprise the following day when I found Anna on my doorstep in tears, holding the dark green dress in her hands so delicately, as though she were carrying a wounded ragdoll.

'Whatever is the matter, Anna?'

'I've burnt it, Reshma! What am I going to do? My husband will be home in two hours and is expecting me to be ready. I can't believe I've ruined it!' she blurted, in between her sobs.

'It's okay, come in, let's have a look.' I took the dress from her, held it up near the only window in our living room and saw the burnt patch – a freshly made hole just by the neckline. It wasn't very big, but it was definitely unsightly, and if she wore it like that, she would certainly stand out at this posh dinner for all the wrong reasons. 'Don't worry, I can fix this,' I reassured her. She stood there in tears whilst I marched off to fetch my embroidery box.

Learning to embroider under my mother's watchful eye back in Pakistan now came in very handy, as I soon got to work and wove some magic – I patched up the burnt area with pastel pink flowers and pale green leaves, adding a few more on each side to make it look like it was part of the design of the dress.

The embroidery gave the dress a unique look and indeed it received many compliments at the works dinner. The evening went swimmingly, as Anna relayed to me the following day when I popped over for one of our afternoon tea sessions.

'Oh, it was wonderful,' she told me. 'We had prawn cocktail for starters, coq au vin for mains, that's a French chicken dish, very la-di-da you know, and a delicious black forest gateau for afters, oh, and there was a cheese board too. But that's not even the best bit because guess what – they have offered my husband a promotion.'

'*Mubarak!*' I shouted out.

'Now then, don't tell me, that means *well done*, doesn't it?' Anna asked.

'Very close – it means congratulations.'

'He has been promoted to manager. The only thing is…' Her voice trailed off like the dying sound at the end of a song on the record player, something else we would do when we were together – she would play some Elvis Presley or The Beatles, and I introduced her to Noor Jehan and Mohammed Rafi.

'What is it? I asked, pausing between sips of tea.

'Well, the thing is, we'll have to move away, as he has been allocated to a totally different mill altogether.' I saw a hint of sadness in her eyes as she pushed a strand of hair away from her face.

'Oh, I see. When will you have to go?'

'We're leaving next month…' she paused for a moment, as she must have detected the sad undertones in my voice when I asked the question, and then she tried her best to sound upbeat, '…but listen, we will still meet whenever we can, won't we, and whenever we do, it will always be with tea and cake and samosas, right?'

'Of course,' I replied softly, as we both fought hard to fight the melancholy mood that now filled the air. It was peculiar how such good news could sour the atmosphere and leave us both feeling glum.

I was indeed so sad to see them go. Anna had been my first friend in Bradford, and whilst I went on to make many other friends, she would always hold a special place in my heart. Not only had she been my first friend, she had been my first neighbour, and also been my first English teacher without realising it, as well as my Bradford tour guide, helping me navigate my way around a new place.

The day she was leaving, I recalled an incident in the grocers in the early days of our friendship. I had walked into the shop ahead of her, as Anna popped into the post office for some stamps. This was my first time in the shop. I picked up a loaf of bread, some tea leaves, a bag of sugar and a pint of milk, and headed to the till. The shop owner looked me up and down.

'Are you sure you have enough money to pay for all this?' he asked in his accusatory tone. 'Only, I know what your sort are like.'

Before I could try to summon up an answer whilst standing in a state of mild astoundment, a familiar voice came from behind me. 'And what *sort* would that be?' said Anna, now at the till, leaning over the counter, in her best imitation of Ena Sharples off *Coronation Street*, a programme I would grow to love in years to come. 'Because I will tell you this for nothing; if 'her sort' aren't welcome in here, then you shall no longer have my patronage either. Nor that of the other dozens of ladies from school who frequent your shop before and after the school run as soon as I tell them what you just said.'

'There's no need for that,' he replied, sheepishly. 'I didn't mean anything by it, and my apologies if I caused any offence.'

She kept that stern ice cold look on her face until we were out of the shop, after which we both burst into fits of laughter like a couple of school girls. I knew in that instant that we had a very special bond, and I also knew on the day she left that I would miss her a great deal.

Over the course of time and distance, our lives travelled in very different directions, we lost touch and many years passed without any communication between us. So you can understand my surprise when, over five decades later, I received a call from her son Peter, not so little anymore, now well into his fifties.

'You remember me Auntie Reshma?' he asked.

'Of course I remember you, I accompanied you and your mother on countless school runs, not to mention you used to chase around after that tatty old football between our back yards for hours on end. You were such a good little boy.'

'Well, I'm not sure that's what Mum used to think when I used to let go of her hand on the way to school and run off.'

'How is your mum?' I asked.

'Mum's not been so good recently.'

'Oh dear, I'm sorry to hear that.'

'She's been suffering from dementia for a number of years. She's in a nursing home now. The last twelve months have been awful. She hasn't recollected anyone or anything for months on end, until a few weeks ago, when she mentioned your name. I dug out an old photo album and showed her the picture of the two of you –'

'Which one, the one by your old back door, or the one we took in Peel Park?'

'The one by the back door. As soon as she saw it, she started talking about you and your time together, afternoon teas, samosas, cakes. It was the first time she had been lucid in I don't know how long. So, I decided to try and track you down. Which has been a bit of a mission to be honest.'

'We moved away too, a couple of years after you all left.'

'Yes, but if I had known that you are the very same Reshma who is the founder and owner of Reshma Foods, I would have found you a lot quicker! I see your name on the pickle jars on the shelves and on the frozen samosa packets in the freezer of the supermarket every time I go shopping.'

'Well, my daughter runs the company now, I am more of a silent partner, although she will tell you I'm not silent enough!'

Peter gave a little chuckle down the line, but then his voice took on a slightly more serious tone. 'I was wondering if you could do me a favour?' he asked.

When I turned up at the nursing home, I was shown promptly into Anna's room; a large, airy room, with minty blue walls, and solid oak furniture. She was sat in a high-backed sofa chair looking out of the tall window onto a well-manicured lawn bordered with a variety of trees, including oaks, beeches, some lilac trees and tall silver birches at the back. I sat in the chair opposite, and that was when she noticed me.

'Reshma, where have you been? I have been waiting for

you for ages. I'm gasping for a cuppa.'

The staff member brought in two mugs of tea and put them down on the coffee table that was placed between our chairs.

'Sorry I was so long. But I'm here now.'

'Yes, but did you bring the –'

'Samosas! Yes, of course I did. And I brought along the ginger cake too.'

I took the food container out of my bag, peeled off the lid and placed it on the coffee table. Anna picked up a samosa and took a bite – she closed her eyes and savoured the taste – perhaps not just the taste, perhaps some of the memories that it evoked as well.

She then opened her eyes, looked at me and said, 'How many times have I told you, you really need to think about starting a business selling these things!'

Fire Next Time

Marcia Hutchinson

Leonora leant forward in the scuffed leather armchair, eyes glued to the TV in the corner of the junior common room. She pushed her tortoiseshell glasses back up her nose. The grainy image sharpened on the screen. While other students sat around talking, drinking beer or coffee, she clutched a mug of sweet milky tea. Posters on the common room walls advertised rowing practice, a Greenham Common trip, Anti-Nazi League marches and the Terrence Higgins Trust.

The image lighting up the screen looked both familiar and very different. Leonora's bottom lip dropped open and tears pricked her eyes. She couldn't hear what the announcer was saying because of the JCR chatter, but she could see the ticker tape narration running along the bottom of the screen and the blurry pictures as the camera panned across the Bradford City Stadium, lit up like bonfire night. It was the middle of May. Great gulfing flames leapt from the ancient wooden structure, a backdrop to her childhood. Loss of life was a certainty; many unaccounted for. Leonora and fire had a long history.

She had walked past the hulking building so many times on her way to Manningham Middle School. Although she had only been inside it once, for Ces Podd's testimonial. Her friends — well, the boys anyway — had insisted that everyone had to go. So she alternately clapped and froze in the stands. All the best Black football players of the day were there: Cyrille Regis, Justin Fashanu, Luther Blissett – they formed an all-Black side to raise money for Ces' retirement from the game after a decade and a half at Bradford.

To Leonora it was just a football match, 22 grown men and what have you, but the guys carried on like they were in the presence of royalty and in a sense they were. She even spotted the great rugby player Ellery Hanley in the stands; she wasn't into rugby but he *was* a proper superstar and very good-looking with it. This same half-familiar space now turned into an inferno?

Noah, who had been sitting on the floor near her feet, turned to her. Like Leonora, he was studying law but he was a rugger bugger, not someone she talked to much outside tutorials.

'Aren't you from Bradford, Leo?'

She nodded, temporarily unable to speak. She rubbed her hands together wincing slightly at the uneven skin on the palm of her right hand, the memories she thought she had long since banished.

'Alright Leo?' Noah asked, his ruddy face creasing. She wished he would shut up because other students were now turning to look at her and she realised with horror that tears had escaped from her eyes and were tentatively making their way down her cheeks. She wanted to tell him that she was fine and could he please mind his own business and not call her bloody *Leo*, but she couldn't trust herself to speak. Opening her mouth would mean inhaling acrid choking smoke that suddenly felt real. She made her escape and headed to the payphone in the Porter's Lodge to call home. No one answered.

As she crossed Old Quad, she saw groups of students gathered lazily in the sun, some poring over books, revising for finals, barely a month away. This was Leonora's last term at

Oxford, after that law school in Leeds and then a job at the Law Centre in Bradford, right on Manningham Lane, less than a quarter of a mile from the stadium that was now on fire. Most of the other law students were going to work in the City or to the Bar. It was hard to think of two places that were so physically different from each other. One built of honey-coloured Cotswold stone designed by the best architects of the last thousand years; the other, the inspiration for hymns about dark satanic mills. Flat-faced towering giants crammed along Valley Road slurping water from the canal to make cloth.

Growing up, it felt as if houses had been merely an afterthought, crammed in along narrow streets to house worker ants for the mighty mills. And the smell: oil, lanolin, grease. Everything was covered in a fine layer of grease, even her asthmatic lungs. Her parents had come to Bradford in the 1950s after the war at the behest of a narcissistic Mother Country. Her father came first, got a job in a foundry and saved up and sent for her mother who worked in the newly-formed NHS, at Bradford Royal Infirmary. She had wanted to be a nurse like she had been in Jamaica but there was a problem with her paperwork. For some reason, her qualifications were not acceptable. She got tired of being pushed from pillar to post so she took the job they had originally offered her, as a cook.

Leonora sat, this time in another leather armchair, slightly less scruffy than the one in the JCR, this specimen was in the corner of her sitting room. Staircase eleven, room three. Although XI:III couldn't accurately be described as merely a *room*. It was a magnificent *set* of rooms. College rooms varied in size from truncated shoeboxes to palatial, the extremes so great that they were allocated by ballot. For the first time in her life Leonora had been lucky and came near the top of the ballot, high enough to get a sitting room, bedroom and, the holy grail, a private bathroom. The oak panelled sitting room had a fireplace and two plump but old leather sofas; a bay window looking out through leaded glass onto Old Quad and a heavy oak door that always took effort to open. Even as she tried to luxuriate in her own private claw-footed roll top bath, she never felt entirely comfortable in this space.

As the water cooled, her mind drifted back to Bradford and her family in their cramped terrace house off Manningham Lane hemmed in on one side by mills of a distinctly satanic variety and on the other by Bradford City Stadium. On match days they could hear the chanting almost as if it was coming from inside the house, and knew goals had been scored even before they were announced on the radio. Their house wasn't close enough to the stadium, she hoped, to be affected by the fire, but what if it spread?

She topped up her bath with hot water and let her mind drift back four years to August 1981, when she and her teenage friends were caught up in the excitement of A level results and decisions about where to go to university. After getting her grades, she decided to take a year off and try for Oxford. A place at Durham to study law might have been everyone else's dream but Leonora wanted to aim higher. No one from her comprehensive had ever gone to Oxford and the head of the English department looked at her like she had grown two heads when she suggested it. 'Gillian McAllister didn't get in,' said Mrs Arnold, 'so why do you think *you* will?'

Mrs Arnold worshiped at the shrine of Gillian McAllister who resembled a recent escapee from the Brontë Parsonage up the road. But Leonora was not going to be so easily defeated. She came back to school the next day and talked to the Deputy Head who listened, nodded sagely then helped her fill in the forms. She hadn't even told her parents as she knew her mother would not be happy about this change of plan.

'Lord have mercy pon poor me gyal!' Her mother said when she announced that she was not going to university for another year. 'Yuh ahready have a place. University is university. Is wheh mek you want to go to dis Haxford?'

How could she explain to her mother that Oxford was the

best and she was determined to try, even if it meant spending another year in the crowded family home. She could cope with failing but not trying would be a betrayal of herself.

It was then that her mother confided she desperately wanted Leonora to go to university now, to get away before, like her two elder sisters, she fell pregnant. Surely there was something in between university and teenage pregnancy. But her mother thought only in binary terms: saints or sinners. Leonora said she'd get a job for the year she would be fine. It did not help as far as her God-fearing mother was concerned that the job that she got was as a weekend barmaid at the West Indian Centre. Serving at the bar was not her idea of an ideal job but it paid and would get her through the year.

The Centre was housed on the third floor of Textile Hall on Westgate. On Saturday nights they hired the hall for discos. It was absolutely *the* place to be. All her friends would be there. Gayle, her bestie, short, round and always with a running commentary on everyone else's clothes, hair and makeup, would call for her and they walked along Canal Road into town together. Leonora was a so-so dancer, nothing special but she loved the music and the atmosphere, and most of all she liked watching Lucas. Jazz funk was what it was all about.

He would arrive late, lean against the door post and wait until everyone drank him. He was lean, tall and the colour of dry sand, with cheekbones that could slice Hardo Bread. Because he was Dominican and not Jamaican, Leonora thought him exotic. He and his brother Raphael sometimes slipped into Dominican patois peppered with French words. She knew what *salope* meant but she didn't let on. Lucas was arrogant but the way he danced excused his arrogance. When 'Street Life' came on, he took to the dancefloor like Baryshnikoff, taking his rightful place at the heart of proceedings. His style of dance was astonishing, he could pirouette on one long leg his arms held aloft, and then move to a sinuous hip swaying, while sliding his feet across the polished maple floors, all non-stop seamlessly segueing from one movement to another. You couldn't exactly call what he was doing ballet, but it was certainly close enough to leave everyone mesmerised. For a while, she watched a mixture of *Swan Lake* mixed with Cab Calloway.

Every time Lucas pirouetted he came to a stop with his eyes seemingly on her, but Leonora was not to be intimidated. She stared straight back at him, remembering the first time they had talked. He asked her what she was studying and she told him, listing all ten O levels. He looked at her, his eyes narrowed slightly, he turned on his heel and walked away. What had she done? She found out from Gayle that he was doing five O levels and was considered the clever one in his family.

Why, thought Leonora, should I have to dim my light for a boy? Why were all the ones she knew so insecure that she, with her eaten-a-book-for-dinner, professor-po-face, specky-four-eyed self, was considered beyond the pale. She was probably the only one in their friendship group that knew where the phrase *beyond the pale* came from. She devoured facts like food, but her intelligence marked her out as different not just among her friendship group but among her family as well. She was the one they turned to when anyone needed any help with homework, or her mother needed official letters to be composed. Music, clothes or boys, not so much. She liked all three, she just didn't consider them to be the be-all and end-all of life.

*

She had just finished locking up at the end of the night cashing out the till at the end of her first month as a barmaid. Colson, the Chair of the West Indian Centre Committee, helped her take some of the crates of empty Red Stripe out and down to the back alley. She saw some lads loitering against the building. That wasn't unusual, but what did seem a little odd was that they were wearing bovver boots and olive green silk bomber jackets and their hair was buzzed almost to their scalps.

In the past, whenever her crew saw skinheads, if they were just a few of them, they would run but if they were in a large group they would take them on. Hunt or be hunted. Why was Bradford like this? Why wasn't it possible to walk around as a teenage Black girl in safety? Why did you always have to keep an eye out for skinheads? They had to travel in packs, visit pubs and clubs that were known to be safe. When she went to some of the pubs near her secondary school with some of her white friends from sixth form, she always felt uncomfortable because she was the only Black girl in the group. It never occurred to them that she might feel unsafe and she never told them she did. She laughed and smiled and sipped her cider and pretended that she was having the time of her life in her New Romantic get-up. Would Oxford have skinheads, and if it did would she be able to find a group where she could be safe?

In the wee small hours, her mother woke her angrily to a phone call. She rubbed the sleep from her eyes as she heard Colson ask her if she had locked up properly, there was an unfamiliar edge to his voice. When she asked why, he said there was a fire at Textile Hall. She dressed quickly and headed down to the city centre. The three-storey building opposite Saint John's Market was lit up like an oversized Roman Candle. Four fire engines, and three police cars lent the scene a bizarre carnival atmosphere. Firemen shouted directions and leaned back against powerful hoses. She marvelled at the white spray arcs of water from the fire engines as they tried to tackle the blaze. They got it under control, but by dawn, the third floor where they danced every Saturday night was totally obliterated.

Colson spoke animatedly to the police. A reporter from the *Telegraph & Argus* asked if anyone knew what had caused the fire. A police inspector stepped forward and confidently stated that they could rule out arson. 'How?' asked Colson, 'How you can rule out arson when the flames are not even out yet?'

Leonora took Colson to one side and told him about the lads that had been loitering out the back when she had taken the last of the crates outside. He took her to a police officer and told her to give a statement. She wished she hadn't said anything but she gave a statement and to the best of her ability described the boys.

'You could be describing anyone, love,' said the burly officer dismissively. 'Unless you know them personally that doesn't prove nowt.'

Colson called a meeting the next day. It was held outside, in smoke-tinged cold sunshine, opposite Textile Hall's smouldering, soaked ruins. The building looked like its hair was on fire. With his deep booming voice, he explained that it was ridiculous that the police had ruled out arson before the West Yorkshire fire service had even completed their report.

Weeks later, Colson reported back that even though the building owners had received their insurance payout, a decision had been made not to rebuild the third floor. The West Indian centre had a five-year lease on the top floor. Could someone really have set the fire just to get rid of them? Where were they going to go? Colson was not to be defeated. He seemed to find his purpose in life. Every week they marched and demonstrated and managed to kick up such a stink that they got a Section 11 Grant. They elected a new committee. After eleven men had been elected, Gayle pointed out that a twelve-member committee representing the community possibly ought to have at least one woman on it.

'What about Professor Know-it-All,' said Luke, sniggering and pointing to Leonora. She didn't particularly want to be a member of any committee, but with the building burned down she was out of the job and as a committee member she might be able to make sure she got hired at the new place so she tentatively raised her hand and was elected unopposed. That was how, at seventeen, she became the youngest member of the West Indian Centre Committee and the only woman.

She had never set foot inside Bradford Town Hall before and she was in awe of the dusty corridors, the portraits of the good and great (all male, all white), looking down on her, as she carried papers, books and bags for Colson. She sat through interminable council meetings with him and some of the other committee members as he pointed out that the investigation into the fire had been incomplete at best, incompetent at worst. He talked about things like *judicial review*, and Leonora wondered that if his life had been different would he have become a lawyer? By the end of the year she had gained an education very different from the one at school. They managed to buy a building, just yards down the road from Textile Hall. A meeting was called to give the new building a name, among other things.

'Skeef!' someone suggested, as a new name to be voted on, but they were shouted down as everyone knew it was a derogatory term for women.

Leonora suggested 'Ujima'. She stood and explained that it was a Swahili word for collective work and responsibility. The resulting laughter pushed her back down into her seat. Did she spot a smirk on Colson's face?

Then someone else said, 'Whe bout Checkpoint, 'cos it's where you goh to check for skeef dem innit.' There was uproarious laughter from the boys in the room. Colson nodded sagely and added the name to the others in the hat. When a total of six names had been suggested, Colson called a vote. Checkpoint won handsomely. Leonora and Gayle got up and walked out, accompanied by the jeers of the boys.

That night, in her room, she felt her defeat keenly as she remembered another earlier fire. She had a nightmare about the hellfire that her mother was always telling them would consume them for their sins. When her eyes flickered open, she could feel the heat and smell the smoke, was she in the presence of Satan. All this for not eating her callalo? Surely God had better things to do than burn children who did not finish the food that their mothers worked their fingers to the bone to provide? Apparently not. She breathed in deeply and choked on the almost solid air. Within seconds she realised that she was not asleep and this was not a dream, or if it was, it was a waking nightmare.

There was no one else in the room, just her and the smoke and the Devil trying to claim her soul. She fell to her knees and crawled to the door reaching up with her right hand to grab the brass handle. She heard the crackle and hiss of a sausage dropped into hot oil as her palm wrapped around the red-hot metal. She automatically pulled her hand away leaving strips of skin behind. She tried again this time with the sleeve of her pyjamas. The knob was smooth and round and she couldn't get any purchase unless she squeezed hard. It took everything she had but she got the door open. Dropped to the floor and crawled out. It wasn't nighttime. It was the middle of the afternoon. She was mid nap, the darkness had been caused by the smoke. She got out in one piece, well apart from her right palm. They took her to hospital where she was treated for smoke inhalation. But it wasn't serious. She learned to write with her left hand and her sisters didn't make fun of her crinkled right palm too often. It was the paraffin heater. It lived in the middle of the room throwing out its tainted heat. Somehow it had fallen over and spilled its contents towards the door. Leonora was four. She was blamed for knocking it over. If she hadn't already been burned, her father would have beaten her but there was no need. God had done his work. Leonora and fire had a long history.

Bouncing Back

Bill Broady

...AT ABOUT THIS TIME bears began to appear in the city. My first sighting – a startling orange-brown flash – was at the wheel of a rusty council van that was pulling out – without indicating – from the Shearbridge depot. I watched it in the mirror, closing on me. Its wedge-shaped head, fully two feet wide, was bumping against the roof: neckless, with ring-rolls of jowl fat melting into the shoulders, it vibrated like a blancmange. A matt-black central square – less a nose than a Hitler/Chaplin moustache – was its sole distinct feature. I shaded into the cycle lane to let it pass. The hands on the wheel were swollen, seemingly fingerless: neither flesh nor fur, more like velour. It glanced down and across: in so far as it had an expression, it was contemptuous. Although I could see no mouth, I got the impression that it had said something to me. I gave chase but it shot a red light at All Saints Road to shake me off. Whatever it was, the creature could certainly drive.

I was no stranger to hallucinations. There was an armadillo that I used to have some interesting conversations with and I still always held each new pint of Guinness up to the light to check that the little green lizards weren't once again sporting in its turbid depths. If there was the slightest flicker I'd replace it on the bar and walk straight out: they used to play havoc with my guts, those lizards. And there were more recent spectres that sometimes passed my house: a ragged crone carrying a pineapple and a limping fox-terrier with a child's doll, limbless, in its mouth. I'd yell for Cathy but by the time she got there, they'd always gone. I decided not to mention this latest one and then reminded myself that she'd finally moved out three months ago.

That night I fell asleep on the sofa again, so that by next morning seven hours of subliminal TV images had erased all recollection of the creature. Unfortunately, when I stopped off at the cashpoint on my way to college I saw it again. Across the road, with its back to me, it was staring into a shop window, appraising convertible sofa-beds in chintzy fabrics or, more likely, watching my reflection. Naked, pachydermous, lumpen, it was stumbling in the bondage trousers of its own flesh. At least I could now confirm that it was a man wearing a costume. Then, from north and south, others emerged to join it, greeting each other with broad gestures and muffled shouts. I still wasn't certain that they were bears, though – the flapping, pouchy ears seemed way too long. Not elephants: no trunks. Nor rhinoceroses: no horns. Pendulous, wrinkled: maybe they were bloodhounds? At this point a fourth appeared who actually filled the suit: was it padded out with kapok or was there a real bear inside? So it was bears, then – but what were they doing here? Or, rather, why was I seeing them? As I fled, they had joined hands and were embarking on a clumsy quadrille. The collective noun for bears is a sloth, I remembered, but what about a group of people in ill-fitting bear costumes? – A sag? A slouch? A slump? Driving past the station I saw three more, with proffered leaflets wedged into their paws: the commuters all walked past, unblinking. Obviously, like Orestes with his Furies, the bears were visible only to me.

That morning my students seemed even less interested than usual: there weren't even any embarrassed shufflings when I essayed a joke – dead silence. I'd always liked it when, between ten and midday, the sunlight through the transom window dazzled me but now I sweated, my hands shook, and a series of black and silver circles, like eclipsing planets, floated across my vision. It wasn't the hangover, unless maybe it wasn't quite headsplitting enough. My lecture sounded senseless: as if the good old British Constitution – tacit, unwritten mysteriously insubstantial – was something I was making up, yet another delusion, like the swimming lizards. I wondered if my audience had sneaked away: against the glare I could only make out fuzzy, motionless shapes. I fought off the rising dread that I was addressing a sloth or a slump.

After lunch, I walked back from The Castle with Mal, our Local Historian. He was updating me on his eternal work-in-progress – a vast history of The Bradford Alehouse, which conveniently enabled him to pass off his own alcoholism as research. He'd just discovered exhaustive records in the archives of the size, shape and number of spittoons used in four adjacent Manchester Road pubs between 1869 and 1873. This meant the introduction of a startling new category: IRISH (Genteel). I'd just begun to expound on my startling theory that, wherever and whenever, drink is drink and drunks are drunks when, in front of us, two of the bear-creatures tacked crazily over the mock-cobbles to disappear into the Physics Block. I could have sworn that I'd seen Mal's eyes following them, so I took a big chance. 'What are those things?' I asked, as casually as I could manage. He glared at me – as if I'd propositioned him or, worse yet, contravened every rule of good fellowship. 'The Bouncing Bears' – he doubled up as if something invisible had punched him in the stomach – 'The new campaign to' – he refilled his lungs with air – 'revive the city.' His eyes were unfocusing again: he seemed to be shrinking or, rather, receding, spinning back in his private time vortex towards the safety of 1869 and his spittoons. Perhaps only the past should register in the true historian's visual field? My problem was that I was far too here and now: apart from the odd armadillo, I was strictly limited to whatever happened to be going on.

When I left work at five the bears had massed outside The Mannville Arms. The morning's waddling had given place to capering: only just born, you had to admire the speed of their development. Linking arms, they embarked on a series of high kicks as sickle-smooth as The Tiller Girls, then broke away into hand- or paw-stands. One could even do back and side flips, as if the cracked pavement flags were a trampoline. Each one had its own distinct personality: cheeky, thoughtful, menacing, sad – it was some sort of testimony to the impartibility of the human spirit. They gave off a strong smell, like sour milk overlaid by perfume: I recognised it as Estee Lauder – Cathy used to spray it on our cat. At least I was now secure in the knowledge that everyone else was seeing them too: my students turned their faces away, like they did from policemen, beggars and lecturers.

I drove fast across the city, as if in flight, to The Royal Standard. Betty began drawing me a pint of Taylor's Landlord: had no 'usual' but she somehow always knew what I was needing. The aroma of its herbs unblocked my sinuses with an audible click and I took my first clean breath of the day. A mass of dust motes, like a kindly angel in mid-materialisation, escorted me to my seat. Although no one had fed it, the jukebox began to boom and rattle like an approaching tube train – the opening to Blondie's 'Fade Away and Radiate'. I watched the lights of the traffic bleeding kaleidoscopically through the thick stained glass: poor devils speeding from ghastly jobs to worse homes. I took my first sip of Landlord, lit a cigarette and, closing my eyes, offered up a prayer to my nameless personal god of tobacco, good beer, dust and wasted lives.

I picked up the *Telegraph & Argus*. A screaming headline – *BLAST-OFF!!* – filled most of the front page, with a

BOUNCING BACK

crudely-drawn bear surf-boarding the hyphen from T to O. The subheading ran: *FROM TODAY, WE'RE ON THE WAY BACK UP!* That very afternoon, I learned, Max Madden, the MP for Bradford West, had tabled a Commons Motion congratulating The Council and The Chamber of Commerce on the launch of the Bouncing Back Initiative. Spearheaded by the famous – already! after only a few hours! – Bouncing Bears, its aim was 'to attract the new businesses and tourism that the city so badly needs'.

On the inside pages I read that there were *THIRTY-THREE REASONS TO PUT A BOUNCE IN OUR STEP.* These included that Bradford was now 'The Heart of the Building Society World': did this mean that it contained an unusually large number of such outfits or that – in debt reclamation or mortgage rates – they evinced a higher than average level of compassion?... That Animal Fibres of Eccleshill had developed a revolutionary mix of cashmere and angora goat's wool, to be called Cashgora... That Concorde could now land on Leeds-Bradford's newly-extended runway, although it would admittedly only be appearing on bank holidays to take local worthies – at £1,000 a head – for an hour's Supersonic Champagne Superspin... That Spring Ram were producing one in four UK domestic baths... That we had before us the shining examples of our 'great Bradford achievers', such as Mandy Shires, Joe Johnson, David Hockney, 'King' Kenny Carter – beauty queen, snooker champion, painter, speedway rider.

From every page Bouncer the cartoon bear fixed me with its hypnotic, Manson-like stare. Why was it always saluting? Why was it – apart from a wing-collar and kipper tie – naked? Why did it have no discernible sexual characteristics? Why was it heavily freckled? Why was it strabismic? Could it have been that evergreen school assembly blasphemy, 'Gladly My Cross-Eyed Bear'? I ordered another pint, stopped rationing my cigarettes and tried to make some sense of it.

Bradford, as far as I knew, had no ursine associations at all. It was obvious that, to enlist apt alliteration's artful aid, whatever mascot they'd chosen would have to begin with a B, but why bears? Why not buzzards or bison? Budgies or bandicoots? Why not bantams, the club badge of Bradford City? I supposed that although these were fierce, brave and lion-affrighting, they were also notably ill-fated, being favoured as a parting oblation by Socrates and such... and that recent memories of the Valley Parade fire — of oblivious celebrants in Foghorn Leghorn suits being cauled by the burning stand's molten bitumen cascades — were all too sharp. But why not bats or bees? Bulls or bulbuls? Baboons or babirusas? Badgers, beagles or boomslangs? Why not boars? — A boar's head proudly tops the city's coat of arms, along with the hunting horn of the Rushworth family, who had been gifted Great Horton as a reward for killing such a beast. They don't *bounce*, I supposed, and they weren't cuddly enough. Those tusks might have frightened the children: all they did was rootle and, sometimes, gore. The choice of 'bouncing' was more comprehensible. Alternatives were limited — blooming? buzzing? blithering? blundering? beseeching?... But why 'back'? If Bradford had been away, where had it been? And where was it going? Where was it bouncing from? And where was it bouncing to?

Not even three more pints of Landlord, two packets of cashews or 'California Über Alles' and 'Love-itis' at mind-shattering volume could bring on any further insights. What the hell was it all about? Bradford's goose was cooked by the end of the nineteenth century, when the wool industry had gone into steady and irreversible decline: bear-suits, Cashgora and David Hockney weren't going to change that. There was nothing to be done... But then what did I know? Sitting there, fat and grimy, alone, soaking up toxins — the best I could do was rootle, I couldn't even gore, any more. What had I ever done to attract the new businesses and tourism that we so badly needed? Maybe everyone, everywhere could reinvent themselves by fiat? I was beautiful, I told myself, I was a sixteen-year-old hermaphrodite on another planet... by the look of my liver-spotted hands, the trick didn't seem to have worked. Outside, on the empty streets, I felt a tension in the air as if the silence was about to be broken by the twang of a great bowstring, sending some huge, deadly arrow to strike at someone, somewhere. The dead city was about to be dragged unwillingly back into life: when Christ reawakened Lazarus, I wondered, did he have a bear-suit ready for him? My usual shortcut through the alley behind The Boy And Barrel was blocked by a soft, heaving mass: Bouncer and the others were pouring pints of Tetleys into various gaps in each other's faces. When I finally reached my house – its darkened windows showing that I wasn't home – I had the sudden desire to put my foot down and just drive, drive until I was out of petrol, then get out and run and run... Exit – Pursued By Bears.

I heard that their costumes had been bought as a cheap job lot left over from the last doomed Sugar Puffs promotion, just before their cereal-munching bears had been supplanted by the Honey Monster, a giggling subnormal puppet-hulk wearing a school cap. Whatever, from now on they were omnipresent: in every photograph, always looking somehow awkward and out of proportion, as if they'd been roughly inserted into the places where subsequently discredited elements had, in Stalinist fashion, been airbrushed out. They even appeared flying shotgun in the new three-million-pound police helicopter, the mission of which seemed to be to ensure that our inner-city crack dealing and ram raiding didn't spread to the most isolated and picturesque parts of the Dales. Healthy minds in healthy bodies: they were particularly keen on culture and sport. The corridors of the Central Library were lined with bear colophons, books temptingly displayed in their hollowed-out chest cavities: for some obscure reason, they favoured The Movement – John Wain novels and New

Lines anthologies. Bouncer depped in white tie and tails for James Loughran at St George's Hall, waving a baton in front of the Hallé while they played 'Fingal's Cave', although he appeared to be conducting something quite different – 'Poème D'Extase', maybe. He also regularly guested on tenor sax with the Gordon Tetley Big Band: his solos were admittedly rudimentary, loud and one-note like Rudy Pompilli, but that note was interminably sustained, without a quiver, showing a mastery of circular breathing to rival Sonny Rollins.

Even on our college stationery, the old council logo – grey and black lower case b's merging into a domino mask – had given way to Bouncer, saluting smartly top right or sometimes even, bilocating, in mid-hurtle diagonally across the page, so that you had to fit your words around him. On posters he was represented inflating a word balloon which promoted the council's anti-racism and anti-sexism policies and then – in a second series a few weeks later – he celebrated its non-racism and non-sexism, implying that both these evils had been eradicated in the interval. Bouncer also starred on the AIDS pamphlet that they made us hand out to our students. The text etched on to his sack-like torso, as in Kafka's 'In The Penal Colony', reassured them that 'Bradford's bouncing ahead with its policies and actions over AIDS and HIV'. So we were actually *ahead* on this one: the subliminal message seemed to be that all-over velour was the best prophylactic. Or maybe it was that the bears themselves were infected? Was all that bouncing the first sign of the immune system's breaking down? Were those freckles the telltale skin eruptions? Were their skins' folds and pouches the result of the occupants' rapid weight loss? My students, forewarned, determined never to share a syringe or have unprotected intercourse with a Bouncing Bear.

I finally got to see inside one of them when he was interviewed in mufti on a local TV news magazine. He was anything between 25 and 50: greying, thin and whippy, with angular protrusions from face and hands, as if every bone in his body had been broken and then badly reset. The eyes were strangely distorted, as if full of tears behind pebble glass: he looked a bit like me wearing a talcumed wig and ten stones lighter. His story was familiar but also, as the interviewer informed us, heartwarming: he'd been laid off by Manningham Mills six years ago and wasted away on the dole thereafter. He ate and ate but he didn't get fat; he drank and drank but couldn't get drunk. The more he slept, the more exhausted he felt – finally he was unable even to summon up sufficient energy and will to put a fresh toilet roll in the holder: 'I looked at it all morning, then finally I just put it on top of the cistern'... But now, as a Bouncing Bear, attracting the new businesses and tourism that we needed, his life was back on track. His wife and kids had returned and he'd fully recovered his potency as a husband and his authority as a father. Moreover, he'd undergone a spiritual transformation through the discovery that the animal he was impersonating was, in fact, his totem. 'When I get into that suit,' he said, 'I can feel my bear-soul flowering inside me.' He'd taken his family down to London Zoo, where they'd spent six hours watching the bears: 'They definitely recognised me. They all came right up to the wire and just stared at us, making little whimpering noises'... Poor lad – if they had recognised him it was as a fellow creature trapped in a cage, not as another bloody bear.

Bradford's Bouncing Back: yes, it was perfect. Fighting back would have been too aggressive, implying the unacceptable possibility that we might actually have had some enemies in this world. Bouncing was *le mot juste*: knock us down and we'd rebound straight back off the canvas, not even waiting for the standing count but coming forward only to be decked again. And always smiling, too punchy even to know we were being hit, let alone who was hitting us. After all, we were out to underbid the workers of the third world to attract the new businesses that we needed: 'We speak slightly better American and we're even bigger saps – I mean, can you imagine the sweatshop workers standing for those Bears?'... Bouncer's perpetual salute was also, on reflection, perfect: the Good Soldier without a glimmer of Schweikian irony, the valiant little man ready for orders, cannon fodder, the salt of the earth. Bradford was cringing back, tail between its legs, tongue lolling out ready to lick the hands that were striking it.

In order to attract the new businesses and tourism that we needed, the *T&A* resolutely accentuated the positive. Its political tone changed: no longer did it inveigh – or at least mildly jib – against free market capitalism and government spending cuts. Although the usual local atrocities, disasters and accidents were still reported, these stories were now relegated to the inside pages – starkly factual, shorn of unnecessary details, with nothing of the previous tone of gloomy relish. Feature writers ignored such inconveniences altogether, so you'd read of the two latest murders – wife of husband, son of father – then of the growing incidence of rickets and malnutrition on the Ravenscliffe Estate, then of the torture of animals on a children's urban farm before coming at last to an editorial that asked, 'How can anyone deny that Bradford's Bouncing Back when there's yet another DIY Superstore opening up?'

The moment that anyone did anything marginally noteworthy they were ludicrously over-lauded, installed as instant Folk-Heroes. I'd thought that the whole point of such figures as Robin Hood, Dick Turpin or City's last great centre-forward, Bobby Campbell, was that they had to be nominated by The Folk, not foisted on them by journalists. The Bradford Achievers – Kenny, Mandy, David and Joe – figured almost as prominently as The Bouncing Bears until it became apparent that to be so designated was a poisoned chalice. Only Hockney, far away in LA, about to embark on an epic portrait series of his pet dachshunds, appeared to escape a speedy and terrible nemesis.

Mandy Shires, Bingley's Queen of Beauty, was the first victim. Miss Bradford, Miss UK, then close runner-up in Miss World – they were about to appoint her as Bradford's Official International Ambassadress – leading the fightback, padded shoulder to padded shoulder with The Bears – when it was discovered that she had once posed topless for the *News of the World*. Once the councillors had established that her nipples had indeed been visible, they sacked her. Broken-hearted, Mandy left for a modelling career in South Africa. Next was Kenny Carter, the World Speedway Champion, a monosyllabic but pleasantly open-faced lad, although he was seldom seen to smile. One night, at his lonely moorland farm, apparently without warning or immediate motive, he took a double-barrelled shotgun and killed first his girlfriend, then himself. It took my neighbour, an avid Halifax Dukes fan, the entire morning to expressionlessly scrape all the KING KENNY transfers off the windows of his car and caravan.

Then there was poor Joe Johnson. The whole city had gone wild when he won the World Snooker Championship. Joe had hitherto seemed to be irredeemably small-time. He had as much talent as anyone – with the most beautiful cueing action imaginable – but, as the sneering Celts and cockneys who dominated the game loved to constantly remind him, he always bottled it. He'd never won a single televised match: the cameras paralysed him. He could feel them sucking his soul out of his body – he'd lose as quickly as possible to get away, to efface himself...Then, all of a sudden, the nerves disappeared, prompting rumours of hypnosis, religious conversion or, most likely, a switch from Tetley's to Taylor's. Right from the start of the tournament, he'd given the impression that he'd already won it and that the actual playing of matches was a mere formality. Steely, unblinking, playing at three times his normal speed, he slaughtered Steve Davis, the defending champion, in the final... But as soon as he had it all – success, fame, money

– he discovered that he didn't want it. He didn't like having to endorse things, posing with Page Three Girls, opening supermarkets, being the butt of TV comedians' jokes. He hated having to smile: 'I just want to be ordinary,' he said dolefully. I once saw him awkwardly manoeuvring a chocolate-coloured stretch Mercedes down Thackley Main Street. No heads turned: he looked – incredibly, even in his scarlet velvet suit – ordinary. He loathed having to travel: he only wanted to be with his lovely wife Teryl – an affectionate diminutive, I liked to believe, of Pterodactyl... There was only one thing for it: Joe happily reverted to losing every tournament in the first round. Pretty soon, he'd become an unperson for the *T&A*, which started trying to raise the profiles of two fast-cueing young Thais who had recently settled in the area... but, for me, Joe Johnson – in freely choosing failure over success, in snatching back obscurity out of the jaws of celebrity – was an authentic Bradford Achiever, the perfect role model for the kiddies, a hero of negation, our Bartleby.

If the football or rugby league teams managed to string even a couple of wins together, the previously cynical local sports columnists would now pump up expectations. At fourteenth in the table, they'd opine, City were perfectly placed for that big promotion push: really successful sides always like to give themselves a twenty point deficit to make up, they find it concentrates the mind wonderfully. When, on consecutive nights at Odsal, Northern were to play the Australian tourists and City, in the Littlewoods Cup, Brian Clough's Nottingham Forest, there appeared – under twin portraits of Bouncer in the clubs' garish kits – the promise that 'Our Boys are about to tweak the kangaroo's tail and shut Cloughie's big mouth'. Odsal Top – Britain's highest and largest stadium – has its own microclimate: there's usually a strange Cimmerian feel, as if you are entering a different geological age. That night, the torrential rains and the swirling pink and green fog-banks meant that we were not only spared witnessing The Bears' pre-match routines but also caught only intermittent glimpses of Australia subsequently beating Northern 38-nil. Such fixtures are never cancelled because, with the tightness of tour scheduling, they can't be rearranged: the clubs would play through plagues of scorpions rather than lose out on their most lucrative game of the season. Somewhere in midfield, no doubt, the fabled Wally Lewis was working his magic: all we saw was the ball emerging from the murk four times for an Australian winger to flop over the try-line. The linesman kept sneaking on to the playing area, once disappearing for fully ten minutes: the referee had to come over to fetch him in at half-time. Another top night of Bradford sport: I'd paid ten quid for a drenching and the sight of a fat man with a flag running sideways.

The next afternoon I was in Rawson Market, stocking up on my favourite Roma Mix coffee and Black Diamond cheddar. Nobody else was buying anything: just standing and staring at the stalls or at one another. It didn't look as if they cared much about the commercial possibilities of Cashgora or being at the heart of the building society world: they all looked mad or in despair. I was getting dark looks for not being in rags and having the standard number and disposition of limbs – every second person seemed to be crippled. With extreme difficulty, an old man was pushing a wheelchair: its occupant was a youngish woman, her body terribly swollen, with a facial prosthetic that looked as if someone had rammed a pecten into her bloodied mouth. As always, there was a strange sickly-sweet blue-grey mist hanging in the air, like incense and the fumes from a chip pan fire... Suddenly, the bears were there, seeming to charge straight through the crowds as if they were substanceless, wraiths. The leading pair were carrying between them, like a huge chrome funeral urn, the Littlewoods Cup. A breastless, thyroid-eyed girl was running with them, her head thrown back like The False Maria in *Metropolis*, red satin bra and hot pants matching her kneecaps and nosetip. 'Look out Cloughie!' she screamed in a blood-freezing coloratura like 'The Queen Of The Night', 'It's The Bears' cup!'

The skies above Odsal that evening had, astonishingly, cleared. The pitch had been thoroughly churned up by the rugby: through scrying the skids, stud marks and divots, I tried to reconstruct the unseen play in the previous night's game. The ground staff and The Bears, in City's strip of fluorescent rust and dirty yellow, were busily engaged in roughing it up even more. Perhaps Forest's preening aristocrats would stumble in the ruts or reel in horror at the strange creatures – birds or huge moths? – that would periodically batter themselves to death against the blazing floodlights? Or freeze in front of an open goal as they were struck by the sudden realisation that, far above, the stars were in a completely unfamiliar alignment?

The fastest that Forest moved was when they ran out at the start: the ball, treacherously, did all the work for them. Johnny Metgod stood with his domed head bowed, staring fixedly at the ground, as if lost in contemplation of unknowable things: when the ball interrupted this reverie he'd dismiss it with side-footed passes that would trundle 60 yards, provoking a series of abortive interception attempts, before picking up pace to slip perfectly into the stride of another Forest player, clean through. The more City chased and harried the more languid and unerring the opposition became: they sprang up in space like sown dragon's teeth. The man next to me thought that Nigel Clough roamed the pitch because he was terrified of our centre-backs: they lumbered after him but then he'd disappear, leaving them baffled, lost, nowhere. In contrast, Walker and Fairclough not only nullified our strikers but also somehow managed to get forward into our six-yard box to score from open play. The normal laws of space and time seemed no longer to apply. The previous night's merciful fogs did not return: five-nil and they hit post, bar and junction and our keeper, Litchfield, made at least a dozen good saves. My neighbour was in tears: 'They've shown us up.' His flat cap and Ronco big check jacket glittered with enamel badges and silver-wired pennants: with his tiny bright-eyed head bobbing up and down on his shoulders I was reminded of Robert de Montesquiou's jewel-encrusted pet tortoise. 'They should have played in the bear-suits. They've let us down. I thought we were supposed to be bouncing back.' 'Nay,' said his mate, who'd watched the proceedings impassively. 'We were all over The Forest. We fucking murdered them.' The chelonian stopped crying: 'So why did we lose, then?' 'Best team doesn't always win. A few lucky goals on the break. We've never liked playing against defensive sides.' I wanted to hug him: he knew that winning had nothing to do with scoring the most goals but was measured by his own personal standards of effort, heart, worthiness and sincerity. City, therefore, had never really lost, would never really lose. He was, like Joe Johnson, another great Bradford Achiever.

I couldn't remember when I'd last enjoyed an evening as much. There was a real pleasure – way beyond Eros or even Thanatos – in watching us get stuffed. This obviously wasn't the universal view: unprecedentedly, no one – apart from a few Forest fans, trying not to look too pleased – came into The Drop Kick for a post-match drink. They'd all gone straight home. I sat alone in the snug, lined with faded sepia photographs of behemoth pre-war Northern players – Dilorenzo, Gouldthorpe, Spillane – and unnamed munitions workers killed in the 1916 Low Moor Explosion. 'They've let us down... they've shown us up': the words of the tortoise continued to sound in my head. All this Bouncing Back, this pursuit of some impossible regeneration was merely destroying our ability to fail with dignity. For weeks now, asleep or awake, I'd kept imagining that little family at London Zoo, huddled up against the bars, whimpering with the bears. When the mirage finally faded, we'd no longer know who or where we were.

I'd also been thinking about the people behind the great initiative to attract the new businesses and tourism that we needed... the people who had dreamed up, commissioned and recruited Bouncer and the rest... who were claiming that with our baths, our building societies and our doomed Achievers, we were about to buck the iron laws of geography, economics or the gods. I doubted that they'd been shivering out on the terraces that evening to see whether their promises that City were going to shut Clough's mouth were fulfilled. I knew damn well where they'd be: nice and warm at home, hidden safely away up the valleys of the Wharfe and Aire. I imagined myself walking up a long well-raked gravel drive... I imagined the click as the security lights came on – along with tapes of baying Rottweilers – to reveal, beyond the triple garage, a converted farmhouse, its walls sandblasted to honey-gold... I knew that this must be the lair of The Master of the Bears... I peered in at a lighted window, double-locked and heat-sensored... Two children were playing with pale wooden educational toys between the slippered feet of the pater familial, his face hidden behind a newspaper – not the *T&A*. He hadn't even bothered to listen to the commentary on Radio Leeds – the result had been a foregone conclusion, after all: instead, beautiful music was playing – a Mozart piano quartet perhaps or that sublime 'fuck me' bit in Pergolesi's 'Stabat Mater'... His wife – why, under that cascade of ash-blonde hair, had I given her Cathy's face? – was choosing from the wine rack: Burgundy, Beaujolais or Beaune?... People like that always get away with everything and don't feel in the least bit guilty, never even suspect that there is anything for which they could be called to account... 'What's so wrong about bringing hope to the hopeless, harmless fun to the careworn and grim?... What's so bad about attracting the new businesses and tourism that we need?... What's wrong with being prosperous and successful?...' The Bear Master put down his paper and I found that I was looking into my own face – but unlined, calmer, content. And then, with a pitying smile, he mouthed at me through the glass: 'What's so terrible about being happy?'... At closing time the landlord forced me to leave my car in his car park and put me into a taxi home.

Nature abhors a vacuum: in the next few months, although there were still no signs of the new businesses that we needed, there was certainly a sort of galvanic entropy, a frenzied marking-time. Every half-forgotten sidestreet was suddenly adapting itself to the exigences of idleness. A thousand flowers bloomed: multi-coloured signboards pulsed and glowed... *JOBCLUBS, TRAINING CENTRES, SKILL CENTRES, CATHEDRAL CENTRES, CENTRES AGAINST UNEMPLOYMENT, NEW DEPARTURES, NEW DIRECTIONS, NEW HORIZONS...* So much novelty when nothing could change. So many centres when we had drifted far outside any known circumferences. The problem of unemployment, it appeared, was to be solved by treating it as if it were a full-time job. Soon, if there was any work to be done, no one would be available to do it, being far too busy acquiring new skills. Bradford's highly-motivated army of Esperanto-speaking, spot-welding jugglers would be primed and ready to bounce back into an inconceivable tomorrow. Most of these new training centres, though, looked suspiciously still derelict and never seemed to be open: maybe we did have one local success story, after all – POTEMKIN SIGNBOARDS PLC.

Large areas of the city were vanishing, their mills and chapels crumbling to dust at the very downdraught of the wrecking-ball, to be replaced – seemingly overnight, as if they'd been rolled out like carpets – by huge new roads. The Cock & Bottle – inviolately Grade II listed – now sat on a spur in six lanes of largely empty concrete. The heroically-misconceived idea appeared to have been that if you built roads then the cars – bringing the new businesses and tourism that we needed – would just appear, like blue-tits when you hang nuts out in the garden. The lovely old wooden pedestrian bridge – users of which would run the risk of falling through on to the railway lines below – gave way to the cross-valley Hammstrasse, named after one of our twin towns. No one ever seemed to drive on it: the local feeling was that it was reserved for Panzer Tanks. Who had really won the war? I was glad that my father hadn't lived to see this.

Half the city, it appeared, had been stealthily levelled, recalling the Domesday Book's entry for the Bradford area; after the harrowing of The North: 'Ilbert de Lacy has it – and it is waste'. VASTA EST... Then large display boards went up on every vacant site, heralding imminent office blocks, leisure centres, superstores, malls. The designs – enormous glowing Doric ziggurats – were like Albert Speer on a weird retro-Babylon jag. Two tiny figures – a male and a female – were always depicted gesturing in the foreground, like Adam and Eve welcoming their second Eden. None of these things ever got built, of course, although some Asians in Manningham did embark on a mosque, only to lose heart halfway through, leaving the frame, a fast-rusting orange spider. The last few brick chimneys in the valley toppled: the bears seemed to take a particular pleasure in sitting down on the plungers to detonate the charges. I remembered how, as the school bus came down Bolton Road on winter mornings I'd see the smoking chimneys poking up through the mist like the funnels of a great battle fleet bravely setting out for a doomed engagement. All that now remained were the silver organ pipes of the chemical works: whenever I passed them my backbrain would numb and everything would go dotty, a snowstorm of colours like walking into 'La Grande Jatte'.

I realised that Bradford had just lost its only real chance of bouncing back: the wrong buildings had been demolished. We should have turned the bulldozers loose on the CLASP police HQ; on the BT Centre, like the superstructure of a long-scuttled battleship; on the Halifax Building Society, ribbed and noduled like a sex toy for the stimulation of some ghastly alien orifice; and on – above all – the Council's Architects' Department, a brutalist grey slab with permanent damp swathes on its windowless end walls, as if giants had been – with good reason – pissing up against them. Thus cleansed, we could have relaunched the entire city as a historical theme park: 'The Nineteenth Century Experience'. We could even have changed the name: 'Revisit the industrial revolution in hands-on, interactive Worstedopolis'. The old businesses would be transformed into new businesses by being now engaged not in production but in its simulation. Full employment would be immediately restored through faithfully recreating the last great boom of 1873. Once again, the air would have been unbreathable, the cobblestones slippery with suint, the IMR at 60 per cent. All the newly-woven cloth would have to be thrown away unfortunately but not before all the lost souls of Rawson Market had been gifted walk-in wardrobes full of tailor-made kid mohair. Even such irredeemables would have their part to play – as muttering streetcorner fanatics, temperance or socialist. Mal could have been the technical consultant for alehouses, checking the size, weight and distribution of the spittoons: I'd have supervised the dust and smoke effects and taken care of the beer... Instead, once again, VASTA EST... But maybe there was another theme park possibility that might save us? We could all don rags and – cringing against the tourists' camera flashes – pick around the rubble like rats... 'Come to Post-Apocalypse City: A fun day out for all the family...'

Instead, the place teemed with little plans and projects, such as reopening the long-dark Alhambra Theatre or turning the Little Germany area into 'the North's answer to Covent Garden'. So what was the question? Who could see in that ruined district anything other than a terrible warning? Next it was announced that into the gap between The Silver Blades ice rink and the Central Library was to be inserted the new

National Museum of Photography, Film and Television. This completely baffled me: what connection did any of these things have with Bradford? And, further, what was the point of devoting a museum to such evanescences? Its exhibits would have to change daily, hourly, by the minute... Then there was the reclamation project for Undercliffe Cemetery, its riot of Celtic crosses, obelisks and mock-Egyptian temples etched against the city's northern skyline. Although all its paths had been newly concreted and its graves set straight, cleaned, scaled and polished like long-neglected teeth, the tourists we needed still stayed away. 'Unfortunately, of the 120,000 people buried here,' said a spokesman, 'none are famous. What wouldn't we give for a Brontë or two!' What's Ada Gilroy's armless angel against Oscar in Père Lachaise, Marx in Highgate or Kleist in the Wannsee? – in Bradford even the dead let you down. One day I noticed that a large banner – CATCH A MINIBEAST!! – was spanning the cemetery gates. The still-dense undergrowth was alive with schoolchildren brandishing nets, magnifying glasses and specimen jars. One teacher was leading her group away, white-faced or in tears – perhaps they'd happened upon a distressing strain of flesh-eating worm?

There was still plenty of optimism. On TV, I saw our tourism officer, Maria Glot – under a sign, *BRADFORD: SUCH A SURPRISING PLACE!* – addressing the delegates at 'Confex', a conference of conference organisers. 'We're rapidly losing our old negative image because there's so much going on here,' I heard her say. 'We have so many good venues to attract conferences, it's unbelievable.' She wasn't wrong: the city – being nothing but voids – certainly had the room to host every conference in Britain, Europe, The World, The Universe. So that was to be the future, then: a perpetual conference. In this respect, at least, I myself had been – if unwittingly – bouncing ahead: after one ill-advised lunchtime reversion to Black Bush chasers, while I spent the afternoon dry-retching over my waste-paper basket, I could hear the department secretary informing a succession of callers that I was 'unavailable – in conference'.

You can confer – or conference – anywhere. The previous summer Cathy and I had been rudely joined at the top of Beamsley Beacon by a dozen middle-aged men: they were a disgusting sight – nearly as fat as I am now – purple and wheezing in brand-new Gore-Tex, Yeti gaiters and pinching Zamberlans. Huddled between the summit's double cairns, they started to hold a business meeting, taping flow-charts and organograms on to convenient boulders. A. J. Wainwright meets John Harvey Jones. Even after twenty minutes of conferencing, we didn't have the slightest idea of what they could be making and selling. Cathy was particularly disgusted that their unfortunate secretary, struggling with the weight of an enormous silver coffee thermos, was still parodically high-heeled, short-skirted, décolleté. To our great delight, their discussions of downsizing and economies of scale were abruptly terminated by a swarm of rock-wasps – that had earlier fled from our caporal tobacco smoke – now returning, enraged, to chase them down the scree.

Max Madden and the other local MPs continued to leap up in The House on the slightest pretext to hymn the praises of 'the city transformed'. The Bears even descended on London – 'taking our message to the country', as the *T&A* put it, above photographs of them joshing with Prince Charles and Denis Healey. They'd apparently also been roaming the Underground. An old college friend of mine had rung me after a five-year silence: 'I've just been trapped on a peak-hour tube with a bunch of bear-type things shouting about Bradford,' he said accusingly. 'All the way from Embankment to Burnt Oak. They smelt like shit.' I denied all knowledge but explained that it must have been a sloth or a slump, not a bunch.

There was one project that was realised. Two years after

the Bradford City fire, the new stand at Valley Parade was completed. The day before the ground's official reopening, Prime Minister Thatcher appeared in the city. Although her visit had been unannounced, we knew that she was coming when a two-square mile area was cordoned off – not even Bouncer could get through – the sky turned black with helicopters and sharpshooters appeared on the highest roofs. Inside the stand she was photographed, waving a claret and amber scarf, exactly in the middle of the empty tiers of seating. She looked flushed and excited, as if she was watching a game that only she could see: in which a crowd of Margaret Thatchers cheered as Margaret Thatcher continually crossed the ball for the centre forward, Margaret Thatcher, to head into the net – goal after goal after goal. On the smoked glass of the bulletproof Jaguar that brought her was a *BRADFORD'S BOUNCING BACK* sticker. 'Such a good campaign,' she cooed as she left. Even before they hit the M1, I guessed the window would be wound down and a clawed hand would release into the slip-stream a screwed-up strip of cellulose.

Perhaps to restore flagging morale, Bradford's much-loved Christmas lights – dim, fusing and cutting out, tangled round fascia and streetlamps like dying creepers, spelling out indecipherable messages, delineating unrecognisable shapes – appeared earlier than usual this year. We were even having a celebrity to turn them on: Bonnie Langford, the former child star now struggling to resurrect her career as a singing, dancing – sexy, even – all-round entertainer. Unless she married royalty, however, or was unmasked as a mass murderer, she was doomed to be known forever as *Just William* and *The Outlaws*' paramour or anima, Violet – or, as the *T&A* had it, Violent – Elizabeth Bott.

The night of the lights was foul, with wind and driving rain and a swirling ochre mist, as if the old gods were descending from Olympus – or Odsal – for revenge. The crowd in the Town Hall Square was tightly packed and silent:

there was an air of expectancy, as if they were waiting for something of massive significance – the return of Arthur, maybe, or the end of the world. Whenever the press photographers yelled at them to smile they duly obliged, some even feebly waving their arms, so as not to disappoint these poor wet lads with their nice cameras, but still remained resolutely silent. It was a gathering that didn't seem to fit into the crowd-typologies of Caneti or Le Bon: the dead crowd, the leaderless, centreless, directionless crowd, the powerless crowd. I was reminded of when Prime Minister Palmerston had come to the city in 1864, at the zenith of its prosperity, to lay the foundation stone of the great Venetian Gothic temple to Mammon, the Wool Exchange. As he'd recently definitively vetoed any Electoral Reform Act, demonstrations and riots were expected. The streets were lined with Peelers and hired thugs but the vast crowd that finally assembled just stood and watched the proceedings in stony silence. The silver trowel trembled in Palmerston's hand: he felt as if his body was being eaten away by the acids of their contempt. He was dead within the year. It was this same eloquent silence that was said to have killed Sir Henry Irving at The Theatre Royal. This was notorious for being the worst House in the land: they'd watched unmoved as he'd raged and raved as Othello and Lear and finally yawned through his protracted death scene in Tennyson's *Becket*. Irving, apopleptic, spoke his own last words in character; 'Into Thy hands, O Lord! Into Thy hands!' But no beatification ensued: no real storm broke outside, nor did the earth gape to swallow his murderers as they mooched off home.

The Bears were circling the piazza, jiving and reeling to the accompaniment of the UK Championship-winning Alliance Conquest Marching Band. As the rain filled their instruments, it sounded as if they were slipping beneath the waves: as a tribute to the Titanic's orchestra, they played 'Abide With Me', then segued through 'Mouldy Old Dough' to what might have been 'Ode To Joy'. The Bears, I noticed, had stopped capering: now they moved in slow motion, like convicts trudging towards some still-distant gulag. Their suits were saturated: one by one they stopped moving, as if petrified by the crowd's unblinking regard. A couple fell to their knees, as if in a final prayer for mercy: stewards in fluorescent tabards carried them away.

Looking disturbingly like Mrs Thatcher in a set of Bugs Bunny teeth, Bonnie Langford – with an electrocutioner's relish – threw the switch. The resultant watery illuminations elicited no cheers: it seemed to grow even darker, as if a black light was seeping out and spreading, like squid's ink. Then Kleig spots revealed The Town Hall's new installation: a 33-foot-high inflatable Father Christmas, clinging precariously to the campanile. It was like a feeble riposte to the colossal pop-eyed reindeer that seasonally back-scuttled Manchester's bigger, better Lockwood and Mawson neo-Gothic pile. The band left off playing and the dignitaries ducked back inside but the crowd still didn't move. The rain no longer fell but now seemed to be coming upwards, as if from sprinklers under our feet. No one appeared to be breathing: even the small children were silent. The only sound was the gale's demonic howling, as it ripped at Santa's scarlet extremities. It took me ten minutes to get out of that square: it was like fighting, in mounting panic, through an overgrown birch wood.

With the wind seeming to come at me from every direction at once, I ran all the way up Manorgate: I badly needed a drink. A large coach was parked athwart the pavement by The Royal Standard, in defiance of the double yellow line. It was covered with dents and scratches, as if it had passed through shellfire: on its side was written, in crude crimson letters of dripping blood, *MYSTERY SIN TOUR*. The pub was – unusually for this or indeed any other hour – heaving with trade: the high-pitched hubbub even drowned out the jukebox. Still more unusual was that it was full of women – and not even those occasional pallid prostitutes on their mid-evening break. These were all dressed in bright, baggy jumpsuits, like chic mechanics; all were slim, extremely clean and healthy-looking, like dental nurses; all had similar short, bobbed haircuts of various shades. And they were all also extremely drunk... or so I first thought before I realised that their extreme animation was something else – sexual excitement? Fear? Anger? I decided that it must be someone's hen night, with the boot, for a few hours, being on the other foot – a couple of red-faced men were hurriedly drinking up and leaving, to loud jeers.

A woman at the bar was ordering 27 pints of snakebite, which seemed an appropriate drink for such maenads. I felt a gentle but firm elbow in my ribs: 'Which was The Ripper's seat?' she asked me. I pointed to the table next to the jukebox. Peter Sutcliffe had apparently been a regular in here during the New Wave days, before they took away its music licence, but try as I might I just couldn't remember him. No one would ever sit in his old place but, for some reason, none of the five subsequent landlords had seen fit to move the semi-eviscerated buffet and the small chipped table that was now so rickety that a full glass placed on it would slide straight off. While I was helping her to distribute the drinks my new friend told me all about their interesting day out on the 'Mystery Sin Tour' of the murder sites of West Yorkshire. They'd spent the afternoon being photographed outside 'The Ripper House', inside which Sonia Sutcliffe was still living: one of them had finally managed to get up the courage to ring the bell – then they'd all run back to their coach but no one came to the door. She and the others were the Rochdale Young Wives Club, meeting up every fortnight for outings and socials. I told her about a similar group in eighteenth-century Paris that I'd just been reading about in Mackay's *Extraordinary Popular Delusions,* who had all killed off their husbands by administering slow poison: she appeared to be seriously taken with the idea. I collected my pint and, although I knew myself to be too old and fat to be worth harassing, hid away round the corner. Didn't people in Lancashire ever kill each other, then? I hadn't realised that Rochdale was such a haven of brotherly love and boredom.

At this point it struck me: here they were at last! The new businesses and tourism that we needed! It was really happening! Before my very eyes, Bradford was bouncing back! The solution had been there all along: we had Third Division Great Men but Gold Medal Monsters. There was Sutcliffe, of course, but also both the Nielsens and Mark Rowntree, the shamefully-underrated 'Stab Spree Schoolboy'... Even Brady and Hindley's moorland graveyard could be reached by a pleasant half-day's stroll along the Pennine Way. Bouncing back would require ruthlessness: the names of the St George's Hall crush-bars would have to be changed – from The Delius and The Priestley to The Ripper and The Panther. Forget the Bradford Achievers and Folk-Heroes: it was time to celebrate those local lads who had followed their dreams, listened to their secret voices, knew that they'd been called, that they were special... I recalled a night in The Flying Dutchman when I was watching journalists pumping the regulars after the seventh Ripper murder. They weren't getting much response until an old gimmer stuck his head out of the Games Room: 'That London bugger, Jack, t'owld one – how many did he do, then?' On being told that it was five he smiled and said, 'Aye well, our lad's beaten yours already,' and returned contentedly to his dominoes and pipe. I submitted that to the *Dalesman*'s 'My Favourite Yorkshire Story' section but, for some reason, they declined to print it.

I'd heard that – as crime increased exponentially, every year bringing new atrocities to be commemorated – Scotland Yard's Black Museum was running out of space. Even with our anticipated confluence of conferences we could still fit them in. The Krays' crossbow, The Black Panther's noose and hood, Denis Nielsen's bath — made by Spring Ram? — and the clear plastic block that held flakes and gobbets of his victims' flesh, the very spade with which Colin Evans buried little Marie Payne (4)... All these things were ours by right. We'd even sired the last three British hangmen: the Pierrepoints of Clayton — Henry, Thomas and Albert — who killed for their country for 55 years. After Henry's debut topping of the anarchist Faugeron, his mentor Reaper Jim Billington had taken the kid's pulse. 'Normal. You'll do,' said Reaper Jim.

Never mind Photography, Film and Television: we'd have the National Museum of Psychopathology! What a money-spinner that would be! The new businesses and tourism that we needed would fly to us like iron filings to a magnet. Think of the merchandising! Think of the spin-offs! I decided that I would make a free gift of this initiative to the city — or at least I would claim no more than a Bouncing Bear's basic wage. We could even keep the current slogan: 'Bradford, Such a Surprising Place' — over a series of portraits of Sutcliffe's thirteen victims, their neutral features staring unsuspectingly back at the camera. We could keep The Bears too: Bouncer, in a stick-on crêpe beard and fright wig would hand out rubber claw hammers and retracting screwdrivers to the thousands of tourists who'd day and night be prowling Lumb Lane ready to spring out on unwary working girls. They'd be prostitutes no longer but paid-up EQUITY members, finding in their writhings and simulated death-rattles a greater job satisfaction than their previous provision of the local gourmet sexual fare — the celebrated twenty-second blowjob with a champagne-flavoured condom. But why merely simulate it? We'd all have to make sacrifices to attract the new businesses and tourism that we needed. 'What do women want?' Freud once asked before providing his own short — six-inch — reply. Well, I've gathered that they're pretty keen on being ineptly fucked by drunken fools, but isn't what they're really after — as all those well-versed in the modernist canon know – a violent death at the hands of a sexual maniac, like Wedekind's Lulu? Looking around, I decided not to embark on a straw poll of The Rochdale Young Wives.

When Sutcliffe finally dies in prison, I thought, his ashes could be brought back to Undercliffe for interment: the *ne plus ultra* – better than any Brontë, certain to attract the tourism that we needed. But what form should his monument take? A marble articulated lorry? Or a vastly-enlarged copy of Bingley's Zapolski grave from which, on a tape loop, would issue God's momentous orders to young gravedigger Pete? Then I thought of the centrepiece of the necropolis: the light grey granite Smith obelisk, like a minatory finger high over Bradford. Joseph Smith had been the person who drew up the cemetery's contracts: the middleman, the gopher, had reserved for himself the prime site. After turfing out his bones we could chisel away the stone until it was reshaped as a lethally-sharpened Phillips screwdriver, Sutcliffe's favoured instrument. Then we could flank it with specially-commissioned statues of his victims, classically-draped in the style of Maillol, in attitudes of admonition or supplication. And the epitaph? Well, Sutcliffe – like Villon, Swift or Yeats – had provided his own: the notice he used to stick in his cab window when nodding out on the hard shoulder. 'In this truck is a man whose latent genius, if unleashed, would rock the nation, whose dynamic energy would overpower those around him. Better let him sleep?' How often had I wondered about the meaning of that final question mark?

As I went up for another pint my buttocks were abruptly pinched hard from left and right simultaneously. I swung round in mock indignation – secretly flattered that my arse at least had proved to be still visible to women who, if I'd ever been to Rochdale, could have been my daughters – but there was no one within touching distance, no one smirking or blushing, no one even trying to look innocent. A man in the front bar, however, was giving me the hard stare: I met the gaze but his frown, like some Tibetan demon's, merely deepened. Then I realised that – not for the first time – in the mirror behind the optics I'd been eyeballing myself. At least that was one fight I might have had a chance of winning. I smiled but the reflection's expression didn't change. The face was a flat slab of tallow-coloured skin, except for its nose, squashed, pitted and strawberry red, and the beautiful Tyrian purple shadows under its hooded eyes.

I noticed that some reckless or oblivious soul had plumped themselves down in the chair by the jukebox. All the smoke seemed to have been somehow sucked across into that alcove, so it wasn't until I got up close that I recognised the figure as Peter Sutcliffe himself. He was dressed as in that best-known photograph taken on his wedding day – in frilly shirt, velvet jacket and floppy bow tie, like a croupier. There was a cigarette packet and a throwaway lighter on the table in front of him, but he didn't have a drink. He looked at me and nodded, so I stopped and came straight out with the question I'd always wanted to ask: 'Pete, why'd you hate women so much?' And he threw his head back and laughed for some time before replying, in that famously incongruous fluting voice, 'Don't be so daft. If I'd hated them I'd have had nowt to do wi' em.' Then he laughed some more while he vanished, back into the smoke. The cigarette packet was empty: I'd have taken the lighter as a souvenir, but its flint wheel was jammed. I had to admit that there was something seriously wrong with me – worse than seeing lizards and phantom dogs. I could imagine all the stuff in Sutcliffe's head – love gone wrong, desire all twisted up into hate and fear – but not in those of well-meaning, socially-responsible Councillors or Members of The Chamber of Commerce. Hacking up thirteen women – the darkest blasphemy against the most sacred of things – was still to me a recognisably human activity... but I couldn't conceive what sort of man could put people into bear-suits and let them be – or pretend to be – grateful.

The Young Wives were beginning to drift away back to their coach. They were apparently planning to stop off for a last drink in Todmorden at a pub near the Leeds-Liverpool Canal where the floating body of a little girl had recently been found. 'It'll be her dad that's done it,' one said. 'It's always the dads that do it.' I knew they'd be coming back here soon... The National Museum of Psychopathology! And why should we stop at that? Perhaps we could even top it with a Holocaust Museum? Although there was virtually no Jewish community in Bradford, we had plenty of Nazis – Esthonian and Ukrainian ex-Sonderkommandos and death-camp guards – hiding out in the quiet sidestreets around the park. Those charming silver-haired old gentlemen would make the most perfect tour guides, while also providing a fresh and challenging perspective. New revisionism: 'It wasn't six million,' they'd whisper roguishly. 'It was twenty million... and counting!' The tourist attraction to outdraw even Disney World: Bradford – the Twentieth-Century Experience. It would have saved us but we didn't have the guts to do it.

Now that the pub had cleared, I became aware of half-a-dozen men hunched over the table by the door. They were ashen, as if the sun hadn't seen their skin all summer, and taciturn even by Bradford standards – expressionless and totally silent. They looked familiar but I couldn't remember where from: I'd never seen them in here before. They lifted their glasses, drank and then set them down again with perfect synchronisation: the levels of their beer dropped at exactly the same rate. Only when one came wordlessly to the bar for a fresh round did I realise: it was the poor devil who'd gone all shamanic inside his bear-suit. They were drinking Hoffmeister, of course: it was The Bears – or, rather, their operators, sloughed of the skins. The cheeky one, the thoughtful one, the sad one... they were staring into space, like a defeated army in an old newsreel, sitting at the side of the road as the victor's tanks roll in. They all took out cigarettes: each one gave the one on his left a light and then, as with one breath, they blew out each other's matches. Nowt had happened: Bradford hadn't bounced back, after all... In less than a minute all my scorn and hatred for The Bears had turned to love. I'd been terrified all along that they might indeed succeed in attracting the new businesses and tourism that we needed... but now that they'd failed they belonged once again to Bradford, belonged once again to me. I wondered if I should remind them that the best team doesn't always win – that the best team is the one that never wins, the one that doesn't even take the field – but I didn't want to spoil their perfect moment. I paid discreetly for their next round, threw back a double Drambuie and left.

I half-expected the silent crowd to be still waiting in Town Hall Square but it was deserted, except for three scruffy men propped against each other like rifles forming a tripod. They were pointing upwards and laughing. I assumed that they were mocking or marvelling at the great inflatable but when I reached them I saw that the roof was empty – perhaps I'd at last learnt how not to register things, like Mal. 'Santa's buggered off early doors,' one of them said. The North Wind had evidently torn it from its moorings and borne it away. 'It went bombing down Thornton Road then split in two' – he mimed a severing up from crotch to crown – 'Half went up the Aire Valley, the other'll be Haworth way by now.' 'No presents this year,' I said. 'Happy Christmas.'

Then the booze hit me. I was laying alongside my car for quite a while, not sure whether I was on my face or my back, whether it was the stars that were twinkling or just broken glass among the cinders. I wondered if I should just stay there and rot: rats, maggots, worms and crows would hurry to my corpse, so that at least I would be attracting the new businesses and tourism that we needed... But then, the next thing I knew, I was driving, cold sober, at a responsible speed – if in a previously undiscovered gear, at once jerky and floaty – down the empty Hammstrasse. The sky had cleared and the pavements were riming up with frost but I was snug and warm in my new fur. My paws gripped the wheel, tighter and tighter... my massive head filled the driving mirror. Dreaming or awake, dead or alive, more than or less than human, I was bouncing back...

Madam Doctor and the Tea Lady

Sairish Hussain

IMAN NEEDS TO GET out of the car. There are only 40 minutes left. Why has she just parked up outside the café and wasted time taking deep breaths instead? Breath isn't going to nourish her. She needs to find food if she is going to survive the afternoon.

She slams the car door shut too hard and marches over to the tea shop she visits on Fridays at noon. When the mosques fill for Jummah prayers, the takeaways on Ingleby Road are quiet. There is plenty to choose from, McDonald's, Subway, KFC, and of course, Mother Hubbard's Fish and Chips. Iman doesn't have time for anything extravagant though. It's the humble chai café she beelines for.

Glancing at her phone, Iman sees that one of the messages is from her mother telling her to drop by after work. She's promised two of her friends that Iman will give them a second opinion. Knee pain and persistent bloating are the ailments. Iman wants to reply and remind her mum that she's not a GP. What she definitely is, though, is double-booked with patients for her shift at St Luke's Hospital, with just an hour in between to drive across the gridlocked city, throw her food down her, find parking around the notoriously difficult Bradford Royal Infirmary, and be ready to tackle another rammed list for her afternoon shift there. She really didn't ask for homework too.

Drop by after work. It sounds almost leisurely. *Drop by.* As if Iman is just floating through her day and has time to make unexpected stops and detours. She throws her phone into the bag.

It's the same lady behind the till who offers 'salaam' as Iman approaches.

'Wa'alaikum as-salaam. Can I please have a kebab roll and a –'

'Kashmiri tea,' the lady says, smiling as she finishes Iman's sentence. She forces a smile back but her mother's text message is still bugging her. Then, the work phone starts ringing too. Iman ignores it as the tea lady continues talking.

'I already started making it,' she says, pulling a carton from behind the till.

One of the healthcare assistants has sent Iman a message to say that the first patient of the afternoon has arrived early.

Can I eat please?

'Fresh,' the tea lady adds, beaming, but Iman is distracted.

'Sorry, thank you,' she eventually replies, tapping her bank card on the reader.

'Take a seat. I'll bring it over.'

Iman practically falls on to an empty table. Head in hands. 30 minutes left. Better get a move on. She starts shovelling the kebab roll into her mouth, barely tasting it. She remembers that she'd promised her sister a phone call on her lunch break. Her pager buzzes. #4128. That will be the ward back at St Luke's Hospital, wondering why no report has been written for the 11.40 patient. It was a particularly difficult one and Iman had wanted a second opinion from a colleague who was too busy to respond.

Iman scrolls through her phone, the personal one, ignoring

the message from her sister (*You on lunch yet?*) and the one from her husband (*Nipping out to the shops on my break, what shall I get for dinner? Let me know*).

Iman doesn't know about dinner. She hasn't given it a second thought, even though it is definitely *her* turn to come up with something. Faisal is an accountant and mostly works from home. He has fixed their evening meal for the past three days. Uber Eats has also been used more times than is reasonable. Both their mothers would be horrified, especially his. The freezer is empty of meal prep containers, curries Iman has prepared in frenzied batches at the weekend. The message from Faisal was from over two hours ago. Iman panics when dots appear to indicate that he is typing again.

??

She has nothing to say and swipes away the screen. The pink tea has been placed on the table. Not that she noticed at first, she was too busy scrolling through mindless TikTok videos of pretty girls showcasing heatless curl transformations, the ringlets cascading down their backs, ten-step skincare routines and outlandish self-care days. She'll never do any of it but watches anyway. She picks up the cup of tea and takes a gulp of the steaming liquid, almost burning her mouth. She coughs and splutters, waving a hand back and forth, almost is if fanning her scorched tongue.

'Bismillah,' the lady says, from behind the till. 'Careful.'

Iman laughs with embarrassment and turns away from her. The phone buzzes again. Not her personal one, though she catches a glimpse of some new messages.

Are you dropping by this evening then? Please confirm.
I take it you're not ringing. I'm going back to work now.
Frozen pizza it is then.

Iman ignores them and picks up the work phone.

Your second patient arrived early too. Both are in waiting room.

She has ten minutes. The chair overturns as Iman leaps to her feet, grabbing her bags, phones and pager, all of which are still buzzing. She rushes out of the door without clearing away her rubbish. Without saying 'Allah Hafiz' to the nice lady behind the till. Without even picking up the chair. She only realises this once she is already in the car and about to drive off. The tyres screech. The now seven-minute drive to the hospital just enough time for Iman to reflect on how many people it is possible to disappoint, in a lunch break cut short.

*

Madam Doctor has just left and not finished her tea. Sakina tuts and shakes her head. The kebab roll is half-eaten too. She clears it away, hating the wastage of food, a sight she has had to get used to ever since starting this job. Today must be a particularly busy day. The doctor lady is never usually so rude, to not throw her rubbish in the bin, or leave without a rushed 'thank you' as she runs out of the door. She even overturned the chair in her haste, her different phones beeping and buzzing. Sakina's ears are still ringing from the sound.

Laila. That's what Sakina has named her. A glamorous name. A princess name. Silly really, she should just ask her what she's called. She would, if the doctor even had a second spare to talk. Dr Ali is all it says on the badge dangling from her waist. Sakina has heard Laila on the phone plenty of times, talking about patients, frustrated with colleagues, asking the person on the other end of the phone if 'doctor so and so' wouldn't mind taking her first one. That the list at St Luke's Hospital overran. She'd pay them back by taking not one, but two of theirs. She should be at the BRI in less than fifteen, no, ten minutes.

On those days, Laila hasn't even had the courtesy to order at the till, but Sakina reassures her with a hand that she knows what she wants. She has only been in the job for three months, two days a week, Thursdays and Fridays, the cleaning shifts at the GP surgery not being enough to cover bills over winter.

Sakina is used to being ignored by doctors. Too important they are, as they strut past, to acknowledge a lowly cleaner. Some of them appear surprised when Sakina speaks to them in English. She does it on purpose so that they know she is Bradford born and bred.

It's varied at the café, because being behind the till means she can't be ignored. Since starting, Sakina has served customers once and never seen them again. Groups of youths who come in the evenings after school and hijack the tables at the back of the shop, leaving behind them spilt karak chai, half-eaten doughnuts, crumbs from cake slices and smashed cartons of samosa chaat, yoghurt smeared all over the tables. They usually leave without a second glance at the 'auntie' who manages the till, their profanity trailing behind them as they exit the doors. And then there are the regulars, like Laila, who breezes in every Friday at noon, Jummah time, the quietest time in the café. She orders the same lunch, sits in the same spot by the radiator, her eating punctured with important phone calls and buzzing pagers, and after approximately twenty minutes, leaves the café calm and serene once more.

Sakina yawns and stretches her arms. She readjusts her scarf. There isn't much else for her to do, the post-Jummah rush will start in half an hour. She's already cleaned the shop twice and prepared the food and drinks ready to be served. Her mind lands on Madam Doctor once more. Observing and making up life stories for her customers is a hobby she never thought she'd be on board with. It is perhaps the only thing that makes her shifts bearable until she can take two buses to her parents' home to pick up her sleeping children.

Laila. Probably early thirties, slender and tall. The only thing they have in common is age, nothing more. Laila wears smart trousers and tucks expensive blouses into them. A long, nude coat sweeps in behind her as she enters the café. A tan handbag with the name 'Mulberry' etched onto it. And her hijab, latte-coloured, like the drinks Sakina makes from time to time, for those who prefer coffee instead of chai, worn in a turban style, the epitome of elegance.

Sakina catches sight of her own reflection in the decorative mirrors which adorn the walls of the café. Her belly protrudes and Sakina quickly drapes her scarf over it. She has never been able to shed the weight, not after bearing her first child. Two more came after that and now, Sakina doesn't have time to worry about her looks anymore. Not like Laila, who is always beautifully put together.

The traditional salwar kameez is not pleasing Sakina either, not like it did this morning when she picked it out. It is bold and patterned, garish almost, with a mixture of blues and yellows. She thinks back to the sophisticated nude tones that clothe Laila's body. The tapered trousers, the blush court shoes, the simple gold chain around her neck. Sakina imagines the same goes for what is underneath the clothes too. The doctor will always be waxed, moisturised, toned and hydrated. And Sakina could bet everything she owned that even Laila's bra and knickers were matching. Just imagine.

Give yourself a break, Sakina thinks, heaving herself up onto the highchair behind the till. It took a bit of time to master getting on and off that gracefully. What else could she expect? A mother to three children. A woman with no education. Working multiple jobs to make ends meet. She couldn't afford gym memberships, fancy health foods or expensive beauty treatments. Sakina wonders if Laila has any children. That clinched waist suggests otherwise. Hopefully there will be a husband on the scene, a handsome, educated one to match Laila's beauty and intellect. Perhaps a fellow doctor? It will have been a love marriage probably. Eyes connecting across a state-of-the-art lecture theatre at a top university, the type Sakina could never picture herself in. Not now anyway. She left school at sixteen with just a few GCSEs to her name, struggling her way through maths and English lessons, praying for the freedom of school-free days. It hadn't led to much.

It won't have been like that for Laila though. Academically brilliant, no doubt. School, college and then university. What a privilege. Being armed with books and pens rather than a ladle and a brush, scurrying around the house, stirring and sweeping, scrubbing and kneading. Sakina imagines what it would be like to be an important person, taking off in the mornings for an important job, car keys twirling in fingers, car doors slamming, a phone nestled between an ear and the fabric of a hijab while hands are occupied with other, equally vital tasks. The excitement of the rush, the barking of orders to other people, supporting staff, all rallying around to attend to *her*, the main event.

Sakina has never been the main event. Apart from maybe on her wedding day, not that she could look back on those pictures, she'd torn them to shreds over a year ago. It had only been a small affair anyway, two seats for the bride and groom placed outside in the courtyard of their family home in Pakistan. The guests from the neighbouring village all sitting in rows on the floor, waiting patiently for the celebratory meal. And Sakina herself, painted in makeup that was three shades lighter than her actual skin tone, too much blusher, and cringey poses that the village photographer made her copy from Bollywood movie posters.

She'd always hated those photos.

Sakina thinks of Laila and whispers 'Masha'Allah' under her breath. She always remembers to invoke the name of Allah to prevent the evil eye. She convinces herself that there is no glint of envy in her thoughts about Laila or any other malice. There is no bitterness about a woman she knows nothing about.

Sakina rubs her forehead, eyes closed. She sniffs.

She knows enough.

Just then, a customer walks in through the door, jolting Sakina back to reality. She slides off the highchair and offers her 'salaam' to the gentleman wanting a karak chai to take away. Other cars are filling up the spots outside the café. The post-Jummah rush has arrived. It is time to get back to work.

*

It is Friday again, and a stupid man doesn't hold the door open for Iman. It hits her in the face because her hands aren't free, they're holding phones. Both of which, she's trying to ignore. Both of which, she wants to hurl across the tea shop or drown in the swirling vats of pink chai up by the till.

Iman woke up agitated. A massive fight with Faisal kicked things off late last night. It was the baby argument again, that Iman wasn't taking it seriously enough. They'd done the engagement party, the big wedding, the honeymoon and now three years had nearly gone by.

'Don't you think you're getting on a bit?'

It was the first time he used that one against Iman. And he was right. On paper, he was perfectly reasonable. If this was movie night with her sister, and Faisal, a character in a film, both women would be on his side. The poor, long-suffering husband. The selfish, prickly wife.

But it isn't. This is her actual life and Iman is avoiding the subject of babies altogether. She is just working and working and working and taking every damn shift possible just so she doesn't have to confront a thought that won't escape her mind. Iman wants a baby. Iman dreams of being a mother one day. She *definitely* wants a baby. But how to explain to her husband, just not with him.

Iman rushes into her usual seat and sits down without ordering anything. There are missed calls from her mother and sister. Missed calls from St Luke's Hospital and the BRI. Her pager is buzzing and won't stop. And then messages from both her family and work.

Sorry about last night, but we really need to talk and sort this out once and for all.

Do you think you can get here any earlier, there's an urgent inpatient before the afternoon list starts?

MADAM DOCTOR AND THE TEA LADY

I guess you won't be ringing me this lunch time, either?

Any chance you'll have time for your mother this evening? Auntie Soraya needs to show you a lump in her armpit.

Water is dripping down her back. There is sweat on her brow, between her breasts, coating the palms of her hands. Why is Iman breathing so loud? *Everyone will hear you*, she thinks. Iman can't see anyone though. The chairs are dancing, the tables, levitating. Her phones are ringing. The beep beep beep of her pager is clanging in her ears. Her chest is tight. The collective disappointment of everyone in her life. Their hands are around Iman's throat. She can't breathe. They're crushing her windpipe. Iman gasps and clutches at her neck. Her fingernails dig into her face.

'Are you okay?' a voice is asking. It's the lady who makes Iman's lunch. She is taking timid steps towards her. Now, she is shooing someone out of the door. Iman thinks it has been slammed shut. A swoosh of a sign being overturned. Next thing, she is sliding onto the floor and breathing loud and fast and fast and loud. Iman can't feel her legs. Iman can't see a thing. There is a sudden warmth and a hand is clasped inside hers, a worried face is hovering over her, there is the recitation of Arabic, a mention of God, someone blows cool air on her head.

'You're okay, it's going to pass, it's going to pass.'

A sound emerges from Iman's mouth.

'Deep, slow breaths, you can do it. Copy me. Slow breaths.'

There is that sound, again. Iman stiffens with fear. It is her own voice. Crying out. Almost screaming.

'Allah is with you. You're going to win, Laila... You're going to win.'

*

'Is there anyone I can call for you?'

'No.'

'Are you sure?'
'Yes.'
'Can I get you some water?'
'Please.'

*

'I'm sorry.'
'Don't be. My son's are much worse, that's how I knew.'
'Oh, okay.'
'How are you feeling now?'
'Getting there. I'm sorry, your shop–'
'Don't worry, they should all be at the masjid anyway.'
'Right.'
'Just focus on yourself. Deep breaths.'

*

'God, my patients are waiting.'
'Yeah, about that. I may have been a bit rude to the person who kept ringing you. I told them you weren't well, nothing else, and to cancel everything.'
'Oh.'
'Should have listened the first time, innit?'
'Hmmm.'
'Sorry, the phone kept going off and... Are you... are you laughing? That's cool. Glad you find it funny... It *was* quite funny. Not gonna lie, felt good doing it.'
'Thank you.'
'What is your name?'
'Iman.'
'Ah. Still a cool name.'
'Excuse me?'
'Oh, nothing.'

★

'Your shop, you'll get into trouble,' Iman gestures towards the closed door. A man has knocked on it and turned away.

Sakina probably will, but this is a medical emergency, whether the owner understands or not, is a different matter.

'Shall we both stop caring today?' she says. 'Your patients and my customers. Zero effs?'

Iman smiles a shaky smile and takes a sip of the steaming chai Sakina has just placed in front of her.

'Sorry about your son.'

'Oh yes, they started about a year ago. I've learnt how to deal with it now. It happens less too, Alhamdulillah.'

Sakina waits before asking the next question. 'What about you? Has it happened before?'

Iman hesitates. 'Twice. Once at home, and once in the clinic.'

'Was anyone around… to help?'

'The assistant took care of me. We were too short-staffed for her to get help. And I swore her to secrecy after.'

Sakina notes that Iman has made no mention of the panic attack that took place at home. Silence follows the revelation. Iman's eyes are darting around, she's biting her lip.

'I should go,' she says, teetering to her feet. 'I need to call work.'

'I don't think you should go on your –'

'I'll be fine, don't worry.'

Sakina doesn't want to pry and says no more. She notices that Iman is clutching her bag close and isn't making eye contact with her.

'Thank you for your help today. And I'm very sorry about all of this.'

She rushes out of the door. Once again, Madam Doctor leaves her cup of chai half full.

★

Sakina has made the wrong tea again.

'I asked for karak, not kashmiri,' the woman snaps.

'Oh, sorry, let me fix that for you.'

She did the same thing three days ago. Today, she has done it twice. She busies herself with pouring the correct chai and offering the customer two cake rusks for free as an apology. She is cutting things too fine and in danger of getting caught. Especially after what happened with Iman two weeks ago. As expected, Sakina was hurled into the back office by the manager demanding an explanation as to why the shop was closed for over an hour at noon on Friday. Where were all the customers supposed to get their tea fix coming straight out of Jummah? She may as well have lined the pockets of the competing chai café just down the road. Sakina tried to explain about the medical emergency, about the customer having a full-blown panic attack.

'Well, it wasn't no bloody *heart* attack, was it?' was his response.

Sakina expected to be fired and on the bus home to collect her children, worrying about where to find another job to survive the rest of winter. Instead, Mr. Manager gave her an official warning before sneering, 'No more Florence Nightingale from now on, please.'

It should have reassured her, but since that day, her head has been all over the place. She felt crippled with shame whenever she thought back to Laila, sorry, Iman, cowering in the corner of the café, on the floor, rigid with terror, suffocating and sweating with Sakina helpless beside her. It wasn't the same as when her young son had panic attacks. She could scoop him up and comfort him. This was different, especially when it was Sakina's bitterness that had caused everything. Sakina, with all her grand delusions about Iman's perfect life, the princess name she had branded the doctor by.

Surely Sakina is the one who had cast the evil eye on Laila, sorry, Iman, to cause her to panic and lose control.

She has been counting down the days, but with each passing Friday, Sakina's hopes are diminishing. If Iman has taken a sick note, it could be weeks before she sees her again. It already *has* been two weeks. Sakina might never see her again, and if she's not careful, then making the wrong tea for customers is also going to get her fired.

The customer seems unimpressed by the cake rusks and is trying to haggle a free rose pistachio milk cake instead. Sakina can't possibly agree to that. Mr. Manager will have her out the door within a second. She kicks herself for getting into this situation, arguing with a woman over cake when the door opens and another customer walks in, nude coat billowing behind her and latte-coloured hijab pinned perfectly in place. She is holding a bunch of flowers awkwardly. Stunned, Sakina hands the milk cake to the complaining customer who shoots out of the door faster than Iman has just walked back in.

'Hello,' she says.

'Hello.'

'These are for you.' She hands over the flowers.

'Thank you.'

A young man comes into the café. He raises his eyebrows at the exchange of gifts taking place before standing in line. Iman turns to Sakina who is holding the beautiful bunch of tulips.

'I just wanted to drop these off to say thank you,' she says, in a rushed tone.

'There really is no need –'

'No, I mean it. Thank you for everything you did that day.'

Iman glances back at the waiting customer. 'I can see that you're busy so I'll leave you to it.'

Suddenly, Sakina is furious. 'Don't you think... we should talk?'

She places the flowers down on the counter. She almost

lost her job because of this woman, received an epic bollocking from her manager, has been having sleepless nights worrying about her, and all Iman can do is breeze in, two weeks later, and try to fob her off with some flowers?

Iman blinks. 'Sure, if you're free.'

'I'm closing in twenty minutes.'

'Oh, I have somewhere –'

'Maybe you can have a kebab roll and a kashmiri tea while you wait?'

'Right. Of course, thank you. But just a tea please, no kebab roll this time.'

Sakina surprises herself as she watches Iman settle down by the usual spot next to the radiator. The way she has just demanded a chat with this woman. She's done with being a pushover, but wonders what exactly she wants from the doctor.

*

'We do Matilda cakes now too and these strange, hybrid kunafa cheesecakes, imported all the way from Dubai, apparently. Have you seen all the rage about Dubai chocolate?'

Sakina is talking while wiping down tables. Iman is nodding along. The tea lady has turned the sign of the door to 'closed'. She did that the last time Iman was trapped here. Trapped she feels again.

She doesn't want to talk. Surely the flowers were enough?

Ever since the incident that day, Iman has barely been able to look in the mirror, knowing that someone is out there, seeing her at her most vulnerable. Iman is the doctor, she is the one who is supposed to take care of others. How could she let this happen in a bloody tea shop? Those moments should have been reserved for her family, the husband that she pretends to be in love with, the mother who suffocates her and the sister who she constantly disappoints. Or the therapist

Iman has been paying 60 pound a session to, who smirks silently when listening to her first world problems about settling in a marriage and burnout from a busy, rewarding career.

There was something about this woman though. The warmth of her hand in Iman's, her voice which enveloped her and felt like the embrace of a long-lost friend, the safety her eye contact provided as she guided Iman through the sobs and gasps, when her windpipe felt as if it was collapsing, when her heart felt as though it couldn't take anymore, and begged to stop. As much as Iman tried to forget about the woman from the tea shop, convincing herself that she would avoid that particular café for the rest of her life, Sakina never left her thoughts.

Well, here she is, sitting opposite the tea lady now, wishing she hadn't stopped off at the M&S in the hospital main entrance to pick up flowers. Wishing she had just stayed away and never run into Sakina again.

Iman is struck with how young she is. A baby face, a pretty face, wrapped in layers of a pilling scarf, a shawl draped around her shoulders, the type that her aunties wore, the ones who harassed her about marriage, and now, about having children. The shawl clashes with the colours of her salwar kameez and Sakina's shoes are black and clunky. Comfortable shoes needed for being on your feet all day, for running to catch a bus.

Iman hates the fact that she never really noticed her before. Not properly, she was just the lady behind the till. Hardly saving the world, was she? Pouring pink chai for customers and helping them choose the right toppings for the little Dutch pancakes that they served. *I wish I worked at a tea shop*, she remembered thinking at times.

'How old are you?' Iman blurts out before apologising straight after.

'Thirty-four,' Sakina replies. 'Just turned thirty-four. What about you?'

Iman tries not to appear surprised that this woman is only a year older than her. It went beyond clothes and style. Iman had spent the last two weeks wondering about the older, wiser, mature woman who had looked after her in her time of need. She wonders what life has thrown at her to make Sakina this way.

'Thirty-three,' Iman says. 'Just turned too.'

Sakina smiles, and Iman finds herself reaching out to touch her hand.

'I'm sorry if it came across, if I, well, if I was rushing earlier. This is all just a bit weird for me.'

'It's fine,' she says. 'It's partly my fault, anyway.'

'What do you mean?'

Sakina sighs, 'You come into the shop every Friday and I, I watch you with a lot of admiration. Beautiful, successful and, and, I always say "Masha'Allah", always. You're dressed immaculately, you're having important phone calls with other doctors, and, well, I must have given you the evil eye, done nazar, and that caused all of this, and now –'

'Woah, woah. Stop. You think you've given me the evil eye?'

Sakina nods, looking utterly ashamed. Iman laughs and tells her that she's got it all wrong. Yes, maybe Sakina had watched her with a glint of envy at times. After all, everyone knows about the evil eye. Iman's mother advised her countless times not to share good news on social media, to hide her travel photos, her qualifying as a doctor, pictures of her wedding until after it was over. Iman's sister warned her too, never to underestimate the power of someone's jealousy and the hand it could have in causing things to fall apart. Not saying 'Masha'Allah' after a compliment was frowned upon.

'You look lovely... Masha'Allah,' people would add hastily. *As God has willed.* Whatever the positive attribute, it was a blessing from Allah and so invoking His name would prevent the evil eye.

'You haven't done nazar,' Iman reassures Sakina, though she looks unconvinced.

'But what happened to you then?' she asks. 'Why did it happen?' Sakina immediately holds her hands up and pulls away from the table. 'Sorry, that's none of my business.'

Iman frowns. 'Then why did you get me to wait for you, you wanted to talk.'

'Well, I just didn't appreciate being handed some flowers. And the way you were rushing out of the door –'

'I'm very grateful that you helped me,' Iman says, irritated. 'But this is coming across as a bit entitled.'

Sakina's face changes. 'Excuse me, I was hurled into the office by the manager –'

'I am sorry about that –'

'How can you be? You never asked. It was just a half-hearted "thanks, here are some tulips, see you later!"'

'Look, I probably didn't handle that very well –'

'I was nearly fired, I'm a working mum.'

'Well, I'm sorry for having a panic attack on you and your manager's time.'

'Wow, that is not fair.'

Iman feels trapped. She can feel the same terror rising in her chest, sweat forming on her upper lip, her face flushing. She can't do this again and starts to gather her things. What was she hoping to achieve by coming here again? She walks over to the door, yanking at the handle.

'It's locked,' Sakina says. Iman continues to pull.

'Let me out.'

'Okay, look, I'm sorry. Can we start over?'

'No. And I didn't have to spend fifteen quid and get you flowers, just to come here and to be made to feel like shit.'

Sakina stands up too. 'Iman, come on. I don't help people and expect flowers or even "thank yous" in return.'

Iman stops yanking. Slowly, they both return to their seats.

'You seem to have made a lot of assumptions about me,' Iman says, arms folded.

'And you probably haven't even given me a second thought.'

Iman gives Sakina a funny look. 'Why are you so angry? Actually, why do *I* make you so angry?' This wasn't the gentle woman she envisaged.

Sakina grimaces, 'I'm sorry.' She holds her head in her hands, remembering how she lashed out at her mother this morning too, just as she dropped the kids off before the school run. She felt awful about it all day. 'It's been one of those weeks.'

'Oh, has it?' Iman says, her voice dripping with sarcasm. 'Maybe you can spill the beans on *your* life instead, and then I can tell you all about mine.'

Sakina takes a deep breath. 'My husband left me. He shacked up with another woman a year ago.'

Iman blinks. Sakina dare not look up at the doctor's face.

'And I'm still consumed by it, the betrayal, the hurt he caused my children, the fact that he got a passport out of me, all of it.'

Maybe this is what Sakina wanted.

Iman softens immediately. 'Wow, okay. I'm so sorry. Is that why your little one has been having the panic attacks? You mentioned that day.'

Sakina nods. 'I've lost friends. Family are sick of me. Everyone thinks I should be getting over it by now. But I'm still stalking him on Instagram and Facebook. Still struggling with managing work and money. I'm exhausted all the time. I shout at the kids too much. The boiler stopped working two days ago and there's no heating or hot water. The plumber keeps messing me around. I snapped at my mum this morning even though all she's trying to do is help.'

She wipes away tears. 'And you thought you were the fuck-up?'

They both laugh. Iman feels helpless, not knowing how to make amends for reacting the way she did earlier. There is a knock on the door. It is a couple.

'Are you open or closed?' They shout through the window.

'Closed,' Sakina calls back. They roll their eyes and walk off.

'My husband is jealous of me,' Iman suddenly says.

'What?'

'I don't want to have children with him.'

Sakina's eyebrows travel further upwards, her eyes widen.

'Actually, I don't want to be with him at all,' Iman laughs. 'Do you know how nice it is to say that out loud?'

'I'm sorry, I –'

'Oh, that's not all. I'm sick of being a doctor, I'm totally fucking burnt out, I should be given a "worst sister in the world" award, and my mother is a pain in the ass.'

The lights cut out in the café. There is just the glow from the neighbouring shops, the KFC from across the road, the traffic lights changing from red to green.

'Good timing,' Iman says, cloaked in darkness.

'Motion sensor,' Sakina replies, meekly. 'Shall I get up –'

'No, leave it.'

Perhaps it was better, to not be able to see each other as they spoke about these things. Sakina sits up straighter in her chair. 'So, shall we tackle the husband first?'

Iman sighs. 'He's wonderful, on paper. Doesn't do any of the things that could put him in "bad husband" category. He'll cook when I'm late from work. He'll buy me flowers from time to time. He's mostly supportive. So, I can't complain.'

Sakina thinks of what to say but can't find anything.

'You must think I'm awful,' Iman says, in barely a whisper.

'No, I don't.'

'Sure you do, after what you've been through with your husband. Now that's a real reason to hate the bastard.'

Sakina listens as Iman tells her about the day of the panic attack in the shop, the fight she'd had with Faisal that morning over starting a family. After three years of marriage, it was time. Secretly, even Sakina could see his point. She had done nothing but adore her husband, but she'd been placated with a false sense of security. Looking back, she should have trusted her gut instinct more. The dismissive attitude he had towards her, his wandering eye, the way he treated her like a stepping stone.

'You should trust your gut,' she finally says, feeling bold. Iman raises her eyebrows.

'Really?'

'There is obviously something, your soul isn't aligned with this. With him.'

'Woah, check you out being all deep. I knew you were wiser than your years.'

They both smile but Iman's turns into a look of despair. 'Imagine what everyone would say about me. I have a beautiful sister struggling to find a decent person to share her life with, I have a cousin struggling to conceive. And then there's me, who has everything and is still not happy.'

Iman's voice breaks. She cups her face. Sakina feels a pang of sympathy. Things were a lot more complicated in the doctor's life than she could have imagined.

'When you said he was jealous, what did you mean?' Sakina asks.

'Sometimes I look in his eyes, and all I see is jealousy.'

'That's interesting, when I looked at my husband, all I could ever see was embarrassment.'

'What?'

'He was the brilliant one out of the two of us. I was uneducated with no prospects when we married. Average-looking too. Then to make things worse, I became an overweight mum –'

'Don't you say things like that.'

'It's okay. It is what it is. He, on the other hand, had so

much potential, the cleverest boy in the village back home. All he needed to unlock that potential was a green card, which I provided. Anyway, I'm sorry, I just butt in there,' Sakina says. 'You were saying about Faisal.'

'Well, if I'm ever the centre of attention at a gathering of some kind, even if it is just aunties showing me their aching knees and strange moles, he'll become moody and withdrawn for days after. People are always heaping praise on me for being a doctor. You know what our people are like, Asians love that sort of thing. Later when we're alone, he'll make comments to put me down. Put me back in my place. Punish me for overshadowing him.'

Iman takes a deep breath, forcing herself to say the quiet part out loud.

'Sometimes I feel like he hates me.'

'That might be a bit strong,' Sakina says.

'I don't think it is. We were never madly in love. Our families knew each other and introduced us. We both settled. He ticked all the boxes on paper, and I just went with it.'

Iman looks up, her face set and determined.

'I don't want children with him. Even if my biological clock is ticking. Even if I never marry again. And I don't care who I disappoint in the process.'

Sakina squeezes Iman's hand. 'I've struggled so much finding my feet after my husband left me. I'm not educated like you, I have three kids to support. If I can do it, so can you. You're a doctor for God's sake, you can do anything.'

Iman cowers in her chair, 'But that's the problem, Sakina, *because* I'm a doctor, people expect me to just deal with everything. But sometimes… I can't.'

'What about your parents? Would they be supportive?'

'My father passed away when I was young.'

Sakina feels a twinge of guilt, in her mind she'd built up an image of doctor parents, coaching their daughter into becoming the same thing.

'My mother will go ballistic if she finds out what I'm feeling. Even thinking about it would send her over the edge.'

'She might not—'

'Oh, come on, Sakina. I have no real reason to throw my marriage away. Not real enough for my mother or all the nosy aunties, anyway. I can't even talk to my sister about this. No one.'

'So, what are you going to do?'

'Throw my husband and career in the bin and flee the country,' Iman laughs.

'Be serious now, what are you going to do?'

They stare at each other with blank faces before Iman finally speaks.

'Now do you know why I had a panic attack?'

★

Sakina unlocks the door of the café, the lights blinding them the moment they stood up to leave. Both their phones are ringing now, Sakina's kids and Iman's husband. Their real lives dragging them back.

'Well, thank you… for another strange encounter,' Iman says, looking amused.

'I should be thanking you.'

'Are we crazy, opening up like this? We don't even know each other.'

'Probably,' Sakina says. 'But sometimes, it's just what you need.'

'Promise to stop stalking that good-for-nothing ex-husband of yours on social media.'

'I'll be deleting Facebook and Instagram as soon as you leave,' Sakina lies, her face reddening. She wished the shop was still drowning in darkness.

'Promise, you'll let him go. And what he did to you. As hard as it is. For your own sake, and the children's.'

'I promise.' Sakina takes a deep breath before speaking again. 'You always know where you can find me.'

'Thank you, and yes, I'll see you on Friday of course, on my lunch break.'

Sakina nods encouragingly, but she's already imagining the conversation she'll be having with the manager tomorrow when she offers her resignation.

'Good luck, Madam Doctor,' Sakina says, placing a hand on Iman's shoulder. 'You're going to win.'

Iman stops and focuses on Sakina. A tear blurs her vision. Two weeks ago, those words uttered by this woman, saved her life.

They embrace. The hug is tight, they cling onto each other, like their lives depend on it. 'I forgot to tell you,' Sakina whispers into Iman's ear. 'But I used to call you Laila.'

'Really? Why?'

Sakina shrugs. 'Before I knew your name. I thought it suited you.'

Iman walks away. She waves at Sakina and forces a smile through her car window, knowing she'll never drink pink chai made by the tea lady again. She'll wait until she gets home before she cries.

Iman starts the engine and sets off, glancing around at the takeaways of Ingleby Road. She wonders where in the city she will lunch on Fridays from now on.

One of Our Own

Ross Raisin

For the 56

A LITTLE BAND OF smokers is standing on the pavement outside the Midland. A couple of them nod hello, moving aside to let him through with his family, into the hotel and up the few steps to the bar – Ruthy pushing the door open for her two to dart inside – where the air is already thick with breath and beer, everyone in their groups stood drinking and talking; every few seconds a seam of laughter, as he scans the hundred heads, coursing through the body of supporters.

'Over there, Dad,' Michael says to him, pointing to the far side of the room, where their lot have filled the whole of one of the deep, red booths. 'You and Ruthy get yourselves sat in. I'll go up the bar.'

Ruthy is trying to tell her brother what Mila and Noah can have to drink, but Michael can't hear her through the noise – he twists round so that she can put her mouth to his ear, listens to her order, then he puts his hands onto his nephew and niece's heads and dials their skulls towards the bar, to come and help him with the drinks.

Tony watches Michael go with Mila and Noah, who are

already badgering him, probably for something different to what their mum said they were drinking, then he follows Ruthy through the crowded room.

'Speaking of!' Little Brian calls once they emerge at the enclave of their family sitting around the booth. One side of the group is lit up in a tube of dirty light from the window above them. They are all looking up at him and Ruthy from around a long table: on one side, Cameron, his girlfriend Daisy, and Little Brian's twins; on the other, Little Brian and Peter – with Big Brian perched at the end, his John Smith's barely touched, leaning in trying to hear through the din.

'What's score today, then, Uncle Tony?' Little Brian says, shifting along to make space for Ruthy, as he takes a seat opposite.

'Four-nil,' he says, to a small cheer from the twins. 'Record crowd, sneak into the automatics, and a promotion party on the Kop. You heard it here first.'

All of them except for Big Brian are in the colours – the twins both in full City strip, socks pulled up high over the knees of their skinny legs. He gives them a wink, and they wink back together, then start to poke each other in the arm, and seconds later they are trying to wrestle each other off the seat – *'Get off me, you bastard!'* – until Peter moves in to put an arm around them both and gently squeezes them into his side so that they stop moving. He hasn't acknowledged him since he arrived, his brother. But it's that busy, the place so buzzing with anticipation and Peter's grandkids playing merry hell next to him, that nobody, apart from the two of them, will have noticed.

'Hey, Uncle Tony...' Cameron has his arm behind Daisy's back, where she is sitting quietly beside him sipping a Coca-Cola. 'Jay Benn's from Low Moor, right?'

'Think so. Why? Who's asking?'

'This muppet,' Cameron says, tipping his beer bottle towards Little Brian. 'Me brother reckons he's from Lincoln.'

'No, no, he's Bradford. Him and Bobby, both Bradford.'

Taking their cue, the twins squirm free from Peter's arm and stand up on the seat to start singing – their tiny, piping voices barely audible above the hubbub: 'He's one of our own, he's one –' Just then, Michael appears from the throng, cradling three drinks; Mila and Noah are either side of him, his standard-bearers, each carrying a pint of beer high in both hands. Michael, hearing the twins' song, joins in:

'Bobby Pointon – he's one of our own!'

As the chant reaches the first ring of drinkers, it is taken up – and at once the chorus is sweeping through the crowd, the whole bar swelling with noise, a den of excitement beneath the empty hotel.

The twins are still standing, triumphant, on the bench seat. Mila and Noah want to get up onto it too, but Ruthy won't let them and they start complaining that it's not fair, while they watch Little Brian try, unsuccessfully, to coax the twins down.

'Alright, boys, get off now. You're treading nuts and whatever crap else onto the seat. Off. Now.'

When they both turn around to waggle their little bottoms at him, Little Brian recruits his dad to help him out and together he and Peter deadlift the twins from the seat and carry them off through the bar, probably to play *Who can spot the..?* at the mural. An impulse moves in him to take Mila and Noah over to join them there – to stand next to his brother and make contact with him through the buffer of their grandchildren – but Mila has beaten him to it, taking Noah's hand and already leading him away through the thicket of legs.

'You alright, Dad?'

Ruthy is looking at him across the table.

'Fine, love, yes.'

'You're a bit quiet.'

'No, I'm fine. We've just got here, is all. I'm only settling in.'

She gives him a smile, pressing her foot softly on top of his under the table.

'Okay,' she says. 'Fair enough.'

He heard her talking to Jane in the kitchen this morning, before Jane went off to work. Heard a bit of it, anyway: Jane asking her to have an eye on him today, keep him right. They stopped talking when he walked in, and in the next heartbeat Noah was running up to him wanting to show him his new Nerf gun.

Ruthy has angled herself towards Cameron and Daisy. She has her attention on Daisy, talking to her, making her feel welcome, included. Daisy says something that makes Ruthy laugh, and Ruthy picks up a peanut from the table to toss at Cameron's chest.

'Well, who knew me little cousin had a cultural side to him.'

'Fuck off,' Cameron says. 'Daisy's one doing it, not me.'

Michael turns round from his conversation with Big Brian. 'What's this?'

'I'm doing this dance thing for City of Culture,' Daisy says. 'Cameron's been helping me practise.'

Michael resists the opportunity to rib his cousin. He's intrigued. 'Can we watch it, like?'

'Yes,' Cameron says, with obvious pride. 'There's a performance in July, at the Alhambra.'

In the kerfuffle of interest that follows, nobody is paying Tony any notice. He takes a long drink of his pint, focussing his mind on the cool, calming sluice of the beer down the chamber of his throat, then he gets up to take himself away.

In the solitude of the toilets, standing in at the urinal listening to the muted ebb and flow of voices on the other side of the wall, he wonders what would happen if he didn't go to the match today. If he snuck off now, how would they react? How long before they register that he hasn't come back from the bogs? No chance of him doing it, he knows, the fuss it would create if he did.

When he has finished his pee, washed his hands, he hesitates by the door back through to the bar. Without much of a thought to what he is doing, he goes into one of the cubicles, and closes himself inside. He sits on the toilet lid. For a minute or two he does nothing, just listens to the sound of his breathing coming back at him inside the narrow stall. 'Come on, now,' he whispers to himself, turning his palms over on his lap, one by one, surveying them. 'Come on.' Then he gets up, leaves the cubicle, and goes back into the bar, to the happy babble of his family. For an instant, as he walks towards the booth, he thinks that Peter's eyes meet his through all the bodies: he sees in them a flash of understanding, of need for each other today, but when he reaches the booth Peter is concentrated on whatever he's talking to Little Brian about, and he realises that he must have been imagining it.

*

They stay put in the bar while half-past two. On the dot, Peter taps his watch, stands up to finish his pint, and leads them out from the booth. It is less busy now, as they follow Peter in a procession through the bar. Most groups have set off already, although there are still some clusters of drinkers with full pints. Some who'll get in another after that, before the walk to the ground. At the top of the steps, Cameron links his arm with Big Brian's. He helps him down slowly, even though Big Brian doesn't really need him doing it, until they are out the door of the bar, where, directly in front of them, two old fellas are walking into the hotel. Cameron watches them come past. When the men reach the foyer, Cameron lets go of Big Brian's arm and grips hold of his hand instead.

'Didn't know it was a meeting day for your lot, Grandad,' he says, grinning as he lifts their hands up together to perform the daft, complicated handshake that he's been teasing Big Brian with, ever since they found out that the Freemasons had relocated their Lodge to one of the hotel's conference rooms, and Cameron had spotted Big Brian chatting to a couple of the Masons one Monday night, on his way back from the toilet before the Sky match against Newport.

The four children run ahead once they come out onto the street. The crowd is gathering now: supporters streaming out of the pubs and through the side streets, joining the advance of people leaving the city centre, moving towards the stadium. He can feel an agitation in his tummy – anticipation, and something else too, a wick of fear, deep inside him. He walks up the hill at the back of the group alongside Michael and Ruthy, her pair and the twins zigzagging all over the wide pavement, yattering away at each other the whole time. Mila points at a flurry of feet moving rapidly past them. She punches the air, yells, 'I'm on three!' For a moment, he is confused, then he spies the claret and amber trainers and he understands the game they're playing. Up at the front, Cameron and Daisy are touching and giggling, in their own little world, away now from the clutch of the booth. Tony lets his gaze fall on his brother a short way in front of him. Peter is in his regular position, between the Brians, looking silently ahead. Tony watches the familiar shape of him proceeding up the slope. He thinks that he can detect a new stiffness in his gait, a slight delay of his left leg with each rotation of his hips to step forward. He's only just gone sixty, is Peter, only four years older than him. But it will be too much for him one day, this walk; too much for all of them, in turn. Although, Big Brian turned 83 a month ago and he's still strong as a pony. The image comes back to him of their dad's birthday party at the Harold – all of the great-grandchildren taking turns to get onto his shoulders as he danced around the function room's sticky floor.

ONE OF OUR OWN

They come past Forster Square. The children scoot across the forecourt to take turns hoisting each other up so that they can see above the wall for a peep of the stadium roof, above the terraced houses and train tracks, carving its place out of the sky. In fifteen minutes, they will arrive at the ground. One by one, they will go through the turnstiles. Peter and Ruthy will take all the children to meet Billy Bantam in his illuminated concrete hutch, while he and Michael queue up at the food kiosk and the Brians wait by the toilets until they all go together for a piss, before today's one-minute silence, and kick-off: four generations of men standing in a line at the metal trough with their pies and burgers steaming on the pie ledges above each of their heads. When they're done, they will join Ruthy and Mila and Daisy – to pass through the dazzling portal of daylight into the stand, where they will file onto their row, 97-107; him and Peter at either end, separated by the length of their family. The seat in the middle, Cameron's, will be empty today so that he can sit with Daisy a couple of rows behind. The thought of that empty seat stays briefly in his mind, until he is carried along once more by the usual pattern of things. It brings them together, the ritual of matchday; makes it easier as well, he knows, to keep the right distances between them. Momentarily, as the group bunches up at the crossing, he thinks about breaking out of line to reach forward and touch Peter on the shoulder, to speak to him. But he doesn't know what he would say, so he stays with Michael and Ruthy, lulled by the steady rhythm of his children's voices, speaking about this and that, and the moment passes.

There's a current of supporters now, crossing over Hamm Strasse, flowing between the car boots and bonnets, horns sounding, Mila sticking her tongue out at one of the mardy drivers. Off to his left, he can see the strand of people still on North Parade, a festival of promotion songs and drums and coloured smoke, a thousand final glasses glinting in the sun.

On the other side of the crossing, Cameron says that him and Daisy are going in one of the shawarma places. A new thing, this, which has started happening this season and that he isn't best pleased about. Nor too, he suspects, is Peter. As soon as Cameron says it, Mila and Noah start clamouring at Ruthy to get one for them – 'But them burgers and pizza twist things in ground are disgusting, Mum' – and all of a sudden half the group is piling into the second shawarma place because the first one is shut for a refurb, and there's only Big Brian and him and Peter, left outside on the pavement.

'They'd better be quick,' Peter says to Big Brian. 'Only twenty minutes while kick-off.'

They wait outside the shop. He watches the rowdy gathering of Fleetwood fans further down Manningham Lane outside the Bradford Arms, and the police horses gliding alongside the traffic, glad that their dad is here; that it isn't just him and Peter.

Little Brian is ushering the twins out of the shawarma shop. 'No, lads, I'm sorry, but they're too much for you – you'll never eat all that before we get to ground.' Both of them are giving out to him, starting to cry. Big Brian steps forward.

'How about we go look at the knickknack man's stall, eh? Get you both a badge? Last day of the season and all.'

They walk off together down the pavement, the twins instantly won over.

Peter is facing away from him. He's watching a teenage Fleetwood supporter goading a copper, asking her for her helmet so he can get a photo of himself in it. The copper is motioning with her hands for the boy to keep off the road, but a posse of them are jumping out now in front of the cars and horses, arms in the air, singing: 'We're gonna fuck your party...' The goading one has taken his shirt off. In the white shock of the boy's tensing body, Tony sees, for a second, the future figures of the twins. He turns back round. Through the window of the shawarma place, the others are still in the massive queue, which loops around all the tables inside, waiting to order their food. Peter stays turned away from him, watching the goings on down the road. He tries to think how long it has been, but he can't be sure. Years, anyway. Last time they spoke for any length would have been the wake, except for odd times since – Wembley; Chelsea a few years after – days they'd forgotten themselves for a spell.

When Marie was first diagnosed, Peter had just carried on as normal – taking his lead from Marie herself, her insistence that nobody fuss over her, both of them bolstered by the doctors' confidence that it could be dealt with simply, surgically. Those few years after the op, Marie as bright and bold as ever, it was as if nothing had ever happened. Not that her attitude changed much even when it came back, until it started to take her. It was Peter that changed. Went into himself. Became quieter, but quicker to temper. The first time he came to Tony for help, he made it sound like it was Tony's fault.

'If I'd been able to spend more time seeing to everything she needs, Tone, she wouldn't have got as bad as she is. And it's not like you'd be that put out, either, is it? Way things have turned out for you.'

The other thing that had come between them: work. That his own business had succeeded while Peter's hadn't; or, more rightly, that it had ticked along for longer, before it went to pot.

And he could have helped, at first. It wouldn't have put him out too badly, before the banks went bust and everything hit the fan and suddenly he was hiding from Jane that he needed to take money straight from the till to pay their own bills before the café's. But it was the way Peter had asked, that bullish, the way he had just expected it. It hadn't even seemed that big a thing at the time, refusing him. Just how it was. Because Peter hadn't let on – none of them had known – the mess he was really in, even before the recession: the custom he'd lost, the mechanics who weren't getting paid on time, the credit cards. By the time all that came out, after Marie had passed, Peter didn't much care anymore. He didn't want helping. He made that clear enough to Tony on the long, hot afternoon of the wake. 'Too late, isn't it, pal? Nothing left to save.'

And the years just crept on. They got older, each made their peace with how things had become. Except, he knows – although he'd never say it to Jane, or to Michael or Ruthy – that it was never about the money, not really. The money just got in the way, put a gulf between them that he had not known how to cross, to give his brother the support he really needed, because he had not known how. That kind of opening up, connection, he'd never known how. If you spend most of a lifetime, forty years, not talking about the things you don't want to talk about, fair makes it hard to know how to begin.

Michael is the first out the shop. Mila and Noah are all up his legs pestering him for chips and strips of meat from his polystyrene box.

'Come on, then,' Michael says, chewing, looking at him, then at Peter. 'Let's be having you all.'

*

The noise of the thickening crowd is merging with the massed voices already inside the stadium when they descend Valley Parade. He can feel his blood quickening as they walk on, past the towers of onion sacks outside the Al-Falah wholesaler, the waft of grease from the hot dog stand under the raised steel curtain of the tyre-fitting workshop. A thunderous crack from inside the stadium makes him flinch, then the announcer's voice bursts over the club shop roof, asking one of today's mascots – the dot of a child in the centre circle, visible past the edge of the main stand – *'Star Wars or*

Avengers?' There is a pause, then a small voice over the tannoy: *'Don't know. Me mum won't let me watch them.'* His heart is still thumping as they join the column of supporters moving around the main stand towards the Kop. Cameron and his girlfriend have seen a friend from school and go to talk to him and his family, while the rest of them wait in a huddle near the corporate entranceway into the stand, glancing at watches, finishing off what's left of their heaps of meat and chips. Through the grubby glass block of the entranceway, he can see the bright sea of colour on the other side of it; for an instant, a blurred face – which he steps forward to see more clearly, but she has dipped her head to look down. There are more people they know coming over to say hello, everyone busy talking, and although he has told himself that he won't, a force is taking him away, now, to the other side of the glass.

He woke up with the anniversary running through his mind, but he had been able to put the thought away, while he slipped into the routine of breakfast with Michael and Ruthy and his grandchildren, the bus, the pub, the walk to the ground. As he stands in front of the memorial now, however, he can feel his guard falling away. The movement and noise all around him is disappearing. The crowd of names on the stone, and beneath them the flowers and wreathes, scarves, letters, teddy bears, photographs, are enclosing him in a silent pocket of time, away from today. He remains there, looking, holding himself together, until it is too much, and he shifts his eyes to the ground. He can see, next to his own feet, the feet of the person beside him. When he looks up again, at the woman, she is gazing so intently at the memorial that she doesn't seem to have noticed him; or, if she has, to care that he is staring at her so obviously.

'I know you,' he says.

She turns her face to him and immediately he feels guilty that he has intruded on her time here. He can see, as well, that she doesn't have the faintest who he is. He watches her trying to place him, getting nowhere.

'I remember you from St Luke's,' he says.

She glances instinctively at the memorial, then looks back at him and laughs. 'Bloody hell, that's forty years ago. You sure it was me?'

He smiles. 'Yes. I were in there long enough. Saw you come in every day.'

She turns once more to the names on the memorial. Through the glass, his family are still eating and talking to their friends. For a short interval, neither him nor the woman speak. He resists the urge to look at her again; not to make sure – he has no doubt that it's the same girl – but he is cautious of visiting the memory of her. Never mind he hasn't thought about her for four decades, he'd fancied her something fierce back then. Not quite the full forty years, in truth: he did think about her for a good while after he was discharged – even tried at one point to track her down, he recalls now, not that it would have come to anything if he had found her, gormless lump that he was at that age. He'd never once even spoken to her in the hospital.

'You were here, then,' she says.

'Yes. Just turned sixteen.'

She nods. Briefly, they are both quiet again. He takes in the huge claret and amber wreath, half the height of the twins, that is resting against the wall on one side of the memorial, donated by Wolverhampton Wanderers.

'If you don't mind me admitting,' he says, 'I had a right crush on you.'

She laughs again. 'I'm so sorry – I don't recognise you.'

'Oh, don't worry, you wouldn't. We didn't meet each other. I just used to stare at you like some bandaged pervert every time you came in.'

It doesn't feel right to ask her who it was that she came to visit, but he is certain that it was her dad. He'd been two beds down from him in J1. He had second and third-degree burns, like him, but his had gone further – over his neck and face, his scalp. She would pay him a visit every day. So would the rest of the man's family, although it's only her that he can remember fully. He remembers too how guilty he used to feel, that he looked forward to her arrival on the ward more than he did to his own family's. She'd bring her dad something in every afternoon she came, straight after school: chocolate bars, cans of pop, the *T&A*. Once – only once – she had looked across at him on her way out, and smiled. The memory of it is so vivid that he can feel himself colouring even now, re-entering the teenage embarrassment of that moment, how intensely he'd wanted to draw the flowery privacy curtain around his bedframe and see to the shameful lump in his bedsheets, but couldn't because he was surrounded by all those men chuntering and farting in their beds right next to him.

She is studying him, his reddened cheeks, and he is convinced that she knows exactly what he is thinking. He looks through the glass to where his family are still waiting for him – Mila and Noah finally with their hands on one of the shawarma boxes; the Brians laughing at something the twins are doing; Ruthy looking his way, quietly monitoring him.

'Waited on him hand and foot,' the woman says, and breaks into another smile. 'Never once thanked me, the tight-lipped bugger.'

'I can remember you at the mealtimes, feeding him.'

He pictures her by the bed with the fork poised in her fingers, like a mother, waiting for him to finish his mouthful – the line of families down the ward, all sat doing the same for their own loved ones, whose hands were hoisted up in slings or too badly damaged to do it themselves.

'I didn't know,' he says, his eyes moving across the list of golden names etched in the stone, as if he knows which one it is. 'I'm very sorry. He were still in the hospital when I got discharged.'

She looks confused. 'Dad?' She shakes her head. 'No, no

– he's still going, grumpy old sod. And I'm still at his beck and call, bringing him things to the home every day like I'm his personal assistant.'

It is his turn to be confused now: that she is here, if he'd survived. But then the reflex comes back at him: why wouldn't she be here? Her dad had been here that day. His life would have been changed by it, and so would hers, same as all of them – and for the first time he takes in, properly, the other people gathered in front of the memorial. Some of them are in groups – families, children, old couples – and some are on their own, silently observing, or closer in to the memorial talking softly to it, touching the stone. He watches as a man about his own age steps forward and kneels before the plinth. The man roots about in a rucksack, then takes out a small bottle of Lea & Perrins, which he places onto the plinth, nestled between two big bunches of flowers.

'No,' the woman says. 'It was my cousin that died.'

He keeps his eyes fixed on the kneeling man, his big, knuckly hands braced on the edge of the plinth. He can sense the woman looking at him, waiting for his response to what she's just told him, but he can't take his eyes off the man and his breath is coming more thickly now, quicker, he can hear it coming out of himself.

'Did you lose somebody, love?'

She puts her hand on his forearm. He tries to get the word out – no – but the sound he makes instead is more like a yelp, as if he has just hurt himself, and he thinks that he is going to have to kneel down, like the man in front of the memorial, because his legs are going and something is pouring up through him that he can't stop. He closes his eyes against it, but he is already there. He can see the small group of coppers moving up the gangways, starting to motion people away, but most supporters not seeing them because they were too absorbed in the match. Only when the smell of it reached him did he realise that something out of the ordinary was going on, before the first plumes of smoke. And then it's all broken pieces, which seemed to him like they must have gone on for hours, a lifetime, but he knows all happened in minutes: people streaming forward down the stand and all the players still on the pitch, looking up, baffled, at the crowd. He had stood up and clambered over the rows of seats, as dark smoke moved like a wave down the stand – people shouting, pressing onwards, dropping into the paddock then trying to climb over the final wall, onto the grass. Scalding bubbles of paint under his palms. The strange feeling of trespass, as he stepped onto the football pitch.

He can feel the woman's hand on his arm, but it is all still playing against the sealed film of his eyelids. One of the players, still in his kit, is hauling supporters up from the paddock – and seconds later he is doing the same, pulling people over the billboards, onto the pitch. A little boy in his City strip, his skinny arms reaching up, looking at him, asking to be lifted over the wall. He drags the boy up and over, then picks him up, carries him through the melee of people and discarded jackets and police helmets to the middle of the pitch, where stretchers are being passed over the heads of the crowd, and an old man with a small girl on his shoulders is moving away from the smoke. A man in a St John's Ambulance uniform is coming towards him. When he has put the boy down on the grass before the man, he turns and looks back at the stand, the whole roof covered in flame, a thick black cloud reaching high into the sky above it, and he collapses onto the hot turf.

There is a bellow from inside the stadium. The woman squeezes his forearm and he opens his eyes. Through the glass, he can see that his family have gone in. He wants to go to them, to be with them now, but he cannot move. He can feel her body close beside him, her hand still on his arm, and he whispers to her, 'Thank you,' although when he does turn round to her, she has gone, and it is his brother standing next to him. Peter looks at him for a moment, gives him a single nod, then turns towards the memorial. For a while, time comes unstitched, as the pair of them stand together observing all the girls and boys, the old men and women, the family names, remembered on the stone. Everyone except the last stragglers from the pubs – running now for the turnstiles – has gone into the stadium. He looks behind him, for the woman, but she is nowhere in sight.

There is the thin, shrill cry of a whistle inside the stadium – and at once the whole world is perfectly still, silent.

His brother takes hold of his hand. A feeling of peace is flowing through him. He looks up at the sky – where he can still see his brother's spotty face, above him, telling him that he is going to be okay. Peter is kneeling beside him, holding his hand on the grass. There is a strange, dreamy pain in his arm and he is aware that his jacket has melted onto his skin, but Peter is there, talking to him, letting go of his hand now – and there is another whistle, and a sudden surge of noise rising from the stadium, a union of voices, beckoning them in.

Aroma. Taste. Sweet. Centre.

Nick Ahad

THE SMELL IS THE same.

Everything else is different.

As I walk through the door, the pull that should be a push door and the push that should be a pull door, it's different. It's all changed so entirely that I look around to check I am in the right place, that I haven't taken a wrong turn now that these streets are so much less familiar than they once were.

Out of the window I see the mill opposite, the lethal blind corner, the landmarks tell me I am geographically in the same place, but inside it is completely different.

The smell is the same.

No, not smell. Aroma.

Smell feels pejorative, somehow negative and there's nothing negative about this place, about here.

Not for me, not yet.

Maybe later, maybe after The Conversation.

Right now, before The Conversation, the aroma is all I sense, and the aroma remains the same.

How to explain the aroma?

It's spices, of course it's spices, complex spices. But as complex as the spices are, they are made more complex, deeper, complicated further by more; the sugary smell of the mithai, the frying paratha and crispy samosa, the thick, pungent kebabs.

There is another aroma mixed into the air – nostalgia, the aroma of that other country that's sometimes called the past. Where I am has the aroma of an actual other country of course: back Home. Although I can only assume that. I can't know for sure, obviously.

A thought enters, beckoned by the aroma: this place smells like a greasy spoon caff if a greasy spoon caff served only fried bread. Sans bacon, sans eggs, sans sausages and black pudding, if all it fried was bread, a good old greasy spoon would smell like this.

Then the aroma would be a smell, I think, not an aroma. Greasy spoon caffs definitely smell. Not like this place.

Why am I thinking of greasy spoons here of all places?

I realise something: that I can come to this place, smell the aroma and my senses transport me to a greasy spoon caff is the exact reason I chose this place to tell him. My senses, my physical body, are smelling spices, paratha, samosa and thick, chunky, meaty kebabs – and my mind transports me to a greasy spoon. It's an internal journey steep and far enough to make the head spin and make my insides churn. To walk in here and be transported by my mind to a greasy spoon makes me feel like Jim Stark, the Rebel Without a Cause, howling at his parents that they are tearing him apart. Holding that kind of incongruity in the body and cognitive dissonance in the mind has to have an effect. If I can find a way to explain that to him, then he might understand why I've done what I've done.

Nobody else here, I think, would know what the inside of a greasy spoon caff even looks like, and certainly not how it smells. The aroma of grilling bacon – and that is undeniably an aroma, not a smell – is alien to everyone else in here. But not me. I know it well. I bet they'd be disgusted if they knew why.

'Yes bro?'

AROMA. TASTE. SWEET. CENTRE.

It still makes me double take. Not outwardly now, I've learned to hide the physical manifestation of my inner raised eyebrow. Having been raised in an environment where a 'please' and a 'thank you' earned you praise and the lack of it earned you a clip round the ear, or at the very least a loud 'excuse me?', the lack of those words in places like this used to make me physically recoil. A question mark would form on my face, a contortion that immediately identified me as someone who shouldn't really be there, someone who didn't belong. Nobody else's eyebrows raised, nor did their eyelids bat when they were asked 'yes bro?' and not 'How can I help' or even a simple 'yes please'.

'Gimme two kebab, two samoseh, one chana puri.' I affect an accent.

Not 'please'. Never 'please', never the word that marks you out as an infiltrator, someone who doesn't really belong. I've been here enough times, watched the other men who look like me, my generation, order their food. It's only 'yes bro' and 'gimme', no thank you, no please.

'Please' is something their dads might have said, but it hasn't been passed down to this generation. Of course, that means the men of my generation won't be passing it down to the ones that follow, but that's a problem for later down the line.

'Warm?'

Save for three years at university and a couple in The City while I worked out just how unsuited I was to a job in The City, I've lived here in This City, My City, Bradford, all my life.

My accent has changed, grown, adapted to the world in which I now move. Evolved? Perhaps, but that word comes with connotations. I can say that my accent is different to how it used to sound, and it's definitely different to the voice asking me if I want my food warm.

I say as little as possible; the less I say, the less chance my accent will mark me out in here.

'Yeah. Warm.'

In Bangladesh locals can spot a British Bangladeshi from 100 yards. Before you open your mouth, before you get close enough for them to see that your shade of brown has been cooked under an English, not Bangladeshi sun and so glistens less than theirs, there's something else that gives us away.

'Londoner Bengalis' we're called over there; there's no distinction between Bradford, Tower Hamlets, Rochdale or Oldham born Bangladeshis: we're all 'Londoner Bengalis' to them. And in Bangladesh, Londoner Bengalis can apparently be as easily separated from true Bengalis, real Bangladeshis – 'organic' my auntie calls them – as a lion can be from a tiger by one simple thing.

Our walk.

There's a 'Londoner' walk that us British Bangladeshis have.

The ability to differentiate Londoner Bengalis from Organic Bengalis, to pick us out, was developed over many years as a way to identify which brown skinned folk are worth targeting by beggars as they emerge into the thick fecund air of Sylhet Airport. That's my theory.

I say 'we' are called 'Londoner Bengalis' 'over there', but I don't really know how true that is of course. I've heard it all second hand, reported by friends who have actually been 'back home'.

I've never been to Bangladesh.

Whenever the idea was mooted by me, my grandma, my auntie, my wider family, that it might be good, fulfilling, somehow important that I see for myself the land that birthed my father, it was always an idea dismissed.

'You don't want to go there, it's a filthy, horrible place. There's no streetlights, barely any roads and it's dangerous. Too dangerous for you. You don't need to see it, I left for a reason,' was always His response.

But then I heard occasional, contradictory tales of what a

beautiful land it was from other uncles, back when I was a little boy and we used to speak to other uncles and aunties. Bangladesh was 'too much beautiful', according to one rasping, slightly terrifying uncle, Mukhit. It was a place so fertile, I was told, that whatever you threw on the ground would grow. It was a land of water and rivers, a place bountiful with fish, which was also the reason why 'our people' cooked such bounty of the seas and rivers so expertly and the reason why we ate fish so enthusiastically.

They made Bangladesh sound magical, beautiful, special. Where he saw a rubbish heap, they saw treasure. Where he saw decay, they told me of fecundity, where he saw danger for me, they saw my heritage.

My whisper-thin connection to the 'too much beautiful land of rivers and fish' felt like a silken spider's web floating in the breeze. How to find solidity in a connection that feels like it could be blown away in the gentlest of winds? And so the land that I was, in a sense, from, a place that I felt and believed belonged to me, I could never grasp. There was nothing of Bangladesh onto which I could hold.

He never understood why it was important, why it mattered and I could never find the words to explain why it mattered so much.

No, that's not it, of course I had the words to explain – I just didn't know how to say them to Him.

I should have said it, claimed the land that is a part of me, whatever anyone in this place looking at me sees or thinks. Maybe everyone feels like they are adrift and alone in a Godless universe, but what if showing me, taking me to, allowing me to experience the place where His journey began, which makes it the place where My journey began, gave me an anchor? Don't you want that for me? Why wouldn't you want that for your son?

I would have said something like that, had I been able to find the words. Whenever I did find the courage to voice my feelings, they only ever came out as a vague wondering if I might one day go and see Bangladesh for myself and what he might think of that.

I stopped asking when I hit 30. I could have made the decision to go myself, of course. I thought about it, but childhood terrors are the ones that linger the longest and He had made me terrified of the place, made me believe that the moment I stepped on Bangladeshi soil and breathed Bangladeshi air, I would be assailed by horrors my cosseted England-borne imagination couldn't even conjure.

I always found a reason to postpone any planned trip.

I walk away from the counter to wait for my food, thinking that my 'Londoner Bengali' walk can't possibly mark me out, not here. We're all 'Londoners Bengalis' in this place. Even so, I wonder, maybe my walk is different from the rest of the people in here? The streets I walk are not the same as the streets the people in here walk. I don't live in the same area, I didn't go to the same school, I don't share their language, I didn't grow up eating the same food. Everything about me is different so anything about me might mark me out as different. Is my walk different?

The man in the small booth next to me looks across as I sit down. He pours thick, gloopy mint sauce onto his kebab and into his plate. So much sauce. He drowns the kebab in the mint sauce, pouring so much into his plate it looks like soup. He puts the mint sauce bottle down and it looks like a turd now sits in a bowl of pea green soup. There is nothing in the way it looks that suggests how good it tastes. No matter the taste, the look he gives me when I sit in the booth next to his is the same as if he'd been presented with a bowl of turd a la pea soup.

Bad smell on your top lip? I ask him. In my head. I wouldn't dare ask out loud.

I'm used to looks like that in a place like this.

The way he looks at me is not the same way he – they –

AROMA. TASTE. SWEET. CENTRE.

look at white folk. They might want to look at Whites in here, in this space, in Their space, with disdain, contempt, derision, but no matter how far from the 1960s and 1970s and the No Dogs, No Blacks, No Irish signs we travel, there is something of the forelock tug and hat-tip that our people had to do back then, that remains. No, they don't look at Whites with disdain, despite themselves, they look upon them with something of a sense of gratitude, appreciation that they have strayed from the beaten path and ended up here, a back street in Bradford where the curry is authentic and the spices complex. Their eyes can't help but see a traveller who has gone out of their way to visit 'their' place and their eyes are forced to look on in admiration.

Nor is the way he looks at me the same as the way he looks at his actual apnay, his people, his Asian brothers. He can see that there's something off with me, something not quite right. My skin is brown, but not brown enough. I talk different. I don't walk right. He can't quite articulate to himself what it is exactly that's off when he looks at me, just that it's something.

I know what he doesn't like, the thing he's seeing that he can't quite name when he looks at me. It's this: I've got a white mum.

He can't place me, doesn't know where I belong. I'm ethnically ambiguous and as the sweat dapples his puffed out cheeks while he shovels a full half of a kebab wrapped in a flaky paratha through his lips, viscous mint sauce coating his thick moustache as he does so, he knows one thing about me: he doesn't like the ambiguity.

Bang. Someone tries to push the interior door open. The pull door. Bang. He tries to push it open again. It's Him. He's here.

'Two kebab, two samoseh, one chana puree,' from behind the counter.

So is my food order.

He walks into the room and he too is hit by the aroma. How long since he has been here, I wonder. He doesn't see me.

'Two kebab, two samoseh, one chana puree.'

The second time of shouting is laced with impatience. The man behind the counter knows it's me, I know he knows exactly whose order it is, because he looked at me the same way the man now eating kebab two of four sitting next to me looked at me when I walked to the counter. Why can't he just bring the fucking food over?

If I leave my table it might get taken, if I leave some personal artefact, my phone, my wallet, when I go to collect the food, that might get taken, what I really need is for him to see me, come save the table while I go and collect the food. He hasn't spotted me; it's a Sunday morning, always a busy time for chana puri.

I wave. He still doesn't see me.

'Two kebab, two samoseh, one chana puree!'

I'm going to have to shout over. I've no idea what to shout.

There are probably options, but it doesn't feel like there are any good ones, not in here.

Mohammed? I could shout his name, his actual name. Only it would be the first time I've ever called him by his name and this is not the moment to do that for the first time in three and a half decades.

Maybe Malcolm, the name he was given by the other men, the white men, who worked in the factory alongside him in the 1980s, the attribution of such a name utterly beyond the comprehension of my childhood mind.

Maybe 'dad'. Maybe I shout 'dad'?

But I've never called him that. It's accurate, it's what all my friends at school called their dads, but I've never said it to him, it's not the word I call him.

Abuji. I've always called him Abuji. The Bangladeshi kids I knew, back when I was a child and knew Bangladeshi kids, cousins mainly, they called their dads 'Abuji'. I followed along, hoping to sound like them.

AROMA. TASTE. SWEET. CENTRE.

I only found out when I was in my teens that 'abuji' means 'daddy', but by then it was too late to change. I was a teenager calling his father 'daddy'. It didn't mean 'daddy' to me, it was just his name. I feel like I've been calling my dad by his name all his life.

If I shout it here, across this room, the others will hear and they will all see exactly what this is. A man in his thirties, brown but not brown enough, calling out 'daddy' to one of their own. And they'll all think 'ah, acha' and they'll all think 'halfcaste' and they'll all think they know me and know my story and know exactly who I am and I'm not willing to let them think that because they don't know me and they don't know my story and they have no idea who I am or what I've been through to become me.

He spots me. I see recognition in my father's eyes.

'Oi, bro, two kebab, two samoseh, one chana puri!' It's laced with pure contempt this time.

I gesture to my dad. I point at the table with my finger then point with my thumb to the counter. It's supposed to communicate 'this is our table, I've saved it, can you come sit here and I'll collect our order'.

I see him deciding if he should go and collect the food for me, save me from any further embarrassment; he's only just walked in and he can see what I've experienced while I've been waiting, the looks I've had thrown in my direction.

There's no way I'm letting him save me. I point once again at the table and head to the counter to collect our food without giving him the option to get to it first.

I take the food from the impatient prick behind the counter. I would remonstrate with him, I would ask to see the manager and I would remind him that I'm a paying customer and expect to be addressed as such. I would do all of those things if I were somewhere else. I'm not. I'm here. And that means I'm not me, I'm someone else. I'm the person I become when I'm somewhere like this.

At the table, my dad.

'Hello son.'

Why does he talk with that accent? How did he learn it? If it was entirely Yorkshire, I'd understand, if it was a thick, heavy Asian accent, I'd understand, but this strange hybrid. It irritates me.

It doesn't normally irritate me, but today I'm on edge.

'Hi, Abuji.'

I'm really good at small talk. It was one of the things I learned in the city, how to chat away about nothing, getting clients comfortable, making them feel at ease. I made some feel so at ease that they would sign over tens of thousands, sometimes hundreds of thousands of pounds. Sometimes they'd sign over their life savings to my company, trusting me to invest the money. I'm really good at small talk.

I realise I have nothing to say, no small talk with the man in front of me, the man of whom I am a part.

'How's work?'

'It's okay, Abuji. Busy. I've been busy.'

I have a silent chuckle when I remember I had almost this exact conversation in a taxi the previous weekend. We have the depth, when it comes to conversation, of a taxi ride.

'Are you still working at the bank?'

I don't *still* work at the bank. I worked for a private investment company, running several portfolios. I've never worked for a bank.

'Yes.'

The jowly mouth breather on the table next to us has finished his four kebabs. With an oil-smeared, fat-fingered hand in the air and a grunt, he summons his next course. He gets table service, of course he gets table service.

Four silver bowls full of rasmalai drop in front of him and a pile of luminous orange jalebi, twisting and turning around themselves, just like his massive intestines I think, quickly followed by the thought; I wonder if he has diabetes or if he's about to give himself diabetes.

I search for a question, but all I can dig up is: 'How's Mum?'

'Fine. She's fine,' is all he gives me.

We've reached the outer limit of our small talk.

My mum's 'fine'.

I sometimes wonder if my mum's a racist. Her parents, my grandparents, granny and grandpa, were massive racists. In a time when racists were really racists, when Farage's grandad Enoch Powell was racisting at his racist best, my dear dead granny and grandpa were proper, old-fashioned racists. The kind of racists that would try to put their white daughter in a bath of boiling water and bleach if they found out she was 'shagging a paki'.

Sorry, not if. When. They were the type of racists who would try to put their white daughter in a bath of boiling water and bleach *when* they found out she was 'shagging a paki'. Inaccurate of course; he's Bengali, but I think the nuance would have been lost on them.

They loved me, their mixed-race first grandson. Loved me like only reformed racists can.

But if you grow up in that environment and if we're a product of our environments, then isn't it very likely that my mum is in fact a racist? And what would a racist mum make of birthing half-brown children? Because, that's the thing about being 'half-brown' or 'half-caste'; while it's kind of difficult to define what you are, it's really easy to define what you're not. Because once you're a bit brown, one thing that is certain: you are not fucking white.

Does my mum regret having mixed-race children? As far as I can tell, she and my dad are still happily married. I know they're still married. But what about the children, as I used to hear casual racists asking my mum in the playground when my brother arrived and was in his pram. I was eight the first time I remember hearing my mum being asked the question.

'He's a lovely colour, but it's him and his brother I feel for. This is the thing with you lasses that went off with Asians, what about the children?'

I vaguely remember my mum's response being a characteristic 'something' off. It could have been fuck, it might have been piss, it was possibly bugger, but it was definitely off. I remember that.

The casual enquiring racist had a point, what about us? Do all mixed race kids wonder if their white parent is secretly repulsed by the tone of their skin? Or is it just me?

I've been silent, thinking about my racist mum. Turns out he can't take the silence either.

'It's different here now. I remember when this place was next door and we all sat at the counter.'

'Me too. I remember the chickens in the yard downstairs.'

He looks surprised. Literally – he raises one eyebrow. I didn't know he could do that, I've never seen him do it. I wonder if that means my ability to do it is genetic, like being able to roll your tongue.

'You remember the chickens?'

Of course I remember the chickens. I remember coming here when my dad didn't have a shift at the factory and mum had finished her cleaning shifts.

I remember walking past the stools where Asian men, fresh – or the opposite of fresh – from a shift at the factory would sit at the high counter attempting to shovel chana puri into their tired mouths with exhausted hands.

I remember turning right through a swinging door at the end of the room, past the sink where people could wash post-meal and down the stairs to a restaurant that, I imagined, was just like back home.

Downstairs in an underground basement there were mirrors on the wall opposite mirrors on the wall so that if you tilted your head just so, you could see into infinity. And the chickens. From the promontory of 2025 it sounds unlikely if

AROMA. TASTE. SWEET. CENTRE.

not impossible. Nobody would believe today that back then there were live chickens in a backyard of a restaurant on UK soil, but they really were there. My memory tells me they were running around the yard, but that feels not quite real, a childish embellishment to the memory. They must have been in crates. But what isn't an embellishment is that there were chickens, they were alive and they were real.

If it seems unlikely even for the 80s, all I can tell you is that it must be like when Pinter saw Len Hutton; another time, another time.

I don't tell him any of this. This man, who I'm sure must want to see it more than anyone else, doesn't get to see my interiority. I've told that story on a second date, the story of the childhood-remembered chickens, but I can't tell it to my father sitting opposite, even though he was also there.

'Yeah, yes I remember the chickens. Abuji, I wanted to tell you something.'

I don't know how to talk to him. It's not that we're 'not talking', it's just that we don't talk, we don't have a passageway for communication open to us. We speak different languages, literally, obviously; he never taught me to speak in his tongue. I don't know why, I think he regrets it now. I'd love to ask him, find out if it's a regret, if he thinks we might be closer if we shared a 'foreign' language, but how can you have a conversation like that with someone with whom you do not share a way of communicating?

It will have to go unspoken. Like all the other conversations I desperately want to have with him, this man who is my blood, whose language I can't speak.

'What is it, William?'

He always uses my full name. I've been called Will since 1989 by almost everyone who knows me, but never once by him.

The rasmalai silver pots are almost empty on the table in front of the moustached, puffed-out cheeks of our table neighbour. One has a slurp of milk swirling in its basin. It's halfway to the moustache and lips when the man on the next table hears my father utter my name. On hearing it, his lip curls. He's heard what he wanted to hear, thinks he knows what it means.

The ambiguity has cleared, he's got the answers to his question about why he didn't like me on sight. I look like this, sometimes, in some lights, I might pass for apnay; but my name is William.

He wipes the milk from his moustache, but not from his chin, with a paper-thin napkin the consistency of rice paper. He chucks the napkin down in the now milk-less metal bowl. It's pure coincidence that it hits and stays in the bowl. He slams his hand down on the table, belches out a 'y'allah' and stands to his feet with a surprising grace.

'Allah hafeez,' he calls as he leaves, a peaceful goodbye laced with disdain in my direction.

Fat fuck, I think, *I hope the jalebi have given you diabetes in that sitting.*

How am I supposed to say what comes next? What are the actual words?

'I'm getting married.'

After I say it, after I say the actual words, a space opens up between us, a space where I feel the distance of the land of his birth from the land of mine. Later, I look it up. It's 4,984 miles from Leeds Bradford Airport to Sylhet Airport. That sounds about right. If I were to measure the distance across the table after I tell him, it wouldn't be far off that, I reckon.

'Married, why?'

I don't know why I hadn't anticipated the question. It's the most obvious one of all, in some ways. Of course that's what he would ask. When you work in finance, you learn to read the markets. All it really means is that you learn to read patterns, habits, shifts, you learn to look at big pictures, my job gave me the ability to see the macro. It makes you think in macros, but when you learn to think in that way it means that sometimes you miss the micro.

'Why? Well. We're going to have a baby.'

This is not just a conversation we've never had, it's a conversation the likes of which we've never had or dared to attempt. This territory, for us, is uncharted. We have no maps.

His face is pulling expressions that I not only don't recognise, but I never thought I would see on this face so familiar. Bafflement. Confusion. Shock. And underneath it all, in his eyes, *why*. Why didn't I know this? Why didn't you tell me? Why can't you talk to me? Why did I raise my son in such a way that he can't say the most important thing he's ever said to me without looking me in the eye.

'Who? Who's going to have a baby?'

'Me and my wife. Future wife. Fiancée.'

'Who is she?'

'Someone I met at uni. She's an old friend, we met up again last year and, yeah, we've got together.'

'What's her name?'

This is the moment. The one that I attempted to practice in the mirror and failed every time. The moment where I tell him the thing that's going to change his world, my world, the world. I don't know how to say it.

In the 1970s, when they got together, it wasn't just my mum's parents who wanted to put her in a bath full of boiling water and bleach.

That they ran away to live in a caravan was, even when I was a child, something I knew was deeply romantic.

I didn't realise until I was older that it was also deeply desperate, deeply sad and the last thing, deeply, you'd ever want for your own children. The pain and sadness that went into that caravan, the shouts of 'Paki lover' that followed them down the street, the graffiti, the dog shit through the door of their first home, the 'what about the kids?' questions, the disdain of the neighbours, the hatred of their own parents, the knowledge that the gradual acceptance that came only at the arrival of grandchildren was reliant only on that, on me, not that the family came to actually accept the union.

They went through it all, the smashed windows, my dad being beaten by National Front thugs while walking home from the factory, the mums in the playground inviting every other mum for a tea but not mine, the birthday invitations that never came to the half-caste kids, the 'fuck off back to where you came froms', all of it. And they came through the other side to the late 2010s when every Christmas advert had a family that looked like ours, a rainbow of acceptance, although the advertisers still preferred a white skinned man with a dark skinned woman, too many sexual undertones for the gender role reversal.

They went through it all.

And now I have to tell him this.

When Oppenheimer carried out his nuclear test in the desert, he and his team had to grapple with the fact that they literally might end the world by dropping the bomb they had built. It's the highest stakes in history. They chose to drop the bomb.

'Her name's Sindhu.'

He looks like he's processing. Looks like he's trying to understand what he's just heard.

He's trying to work out what it means.

'So she's... Where's she from?'

Where you really from? It's a question I've been asked on every date, every taxi ride, standing outside a shop, standing in a queue inside a shop, at the butcher's, the baker's and if I ever went inside one, I imagine I'd be asked it in a candlestick maker's. I never expected a variation of the question to come from where it's coming from now.

'She's from Southall. We met at uni. Like I said.'

'Southall? Is that where her mum and dad are from?'

'Her parents are Indian.'

AROMA. TASTE. SWEET. CENTRE.

Sindhu's having a conversation right now with those parents, telling them our news. An easier one than I'm having at the Sweet Centre with my dad. Here, the mithai is in a glass case behind the counter. Where Sindhu is, the mithai will be on a plate on a coffee table, the one where I sat a year ago, meeting her welcoming family.

'Indian?'

Why the fuck does he just keep repeating what I say?

'She's born here, obviously. But her mum and dad are Punjabi.'

A fresh load of kebabs are brought into the restaurant. The kebabs arrive by the 'load' here.

The aroma fills the air.

It's intoxicating, meaty, spicy. That aroma transports me, takes me to a time when things were simpler, where I held this man's hand, my dad's dark hand, in my own small, light-brown hand in this place.

I feel like I'm back there. It's visceral, it feels real and suddenly, his hand is in mine.

He's gripping my hand in his.

I didn't know how he'd react to what I had to tell him.

I knew, assumed I knew, that he wanted me to marry a white woman, just like he had done. He turned his back on his community, or at least the community turned his back on him when he went and married a goree, even now something hidden and shameful. He hates his people, doesn't he? He doesn't want to be part of their backward, insular world, right? He's as much a visitor as I am these days, these forays into the Sweet Centre something alien to him. Back when we came here more regularly, he was closer to the boy he was, the Bangladeshi boy who came to Britain. That boy is now five, six decades away. He came to the Sweet Centre to feel like he was 'home', but that's not home to the man sitting opposite. The man opposite me lives in a white world, sounds like he lives in that world, he doesn't belong with these people in this place any more than I do.

Surely if I, in his eyes somehow slip backwards, if I marry an Asian woman, then his journey is invalidated. His sacrifices, all that he and his wife, my mother, went through, was for nothing. He made sure his children were a paler shade of white, surely he wants that dilution to continue?

And now to tell him that he's going to have a grandchild that will be maybe as brown as he is, this has to be too much for him to bear. Or so I thought.

His hand squeezes mine. We haven't had any physical contact in decades.

I look across the table. His eyes are a deep red.

'Son.'

The tears are of joy. The tears are of happiness. He's not disappointed. He's not angry. He's not sad that I'm not 'marrying white'; he's not angry that I'm 'marrying brown'.

He's crying tears of happiness.

There's a taste in my mouth. I can taste my own tears. Suddenly the aroma is stronger, pungent with spices, deeper. The aroma of the Sweet Centre comes rushing back in. I smell the kebabs. I thought I'd be leaving here with a bitter taste after The Conversation, I thought once I'd said the words it would end the relationship between me and him and me and this place for good. I thought I'd tell him and he would disown me for marrying an Asian woman, that somehow he wouldn't want that for me, he'd be angry, disappointed. He's none of those things. Not even close.

Now that it's here, the moment isn't bitter. It's sweet.

I know then that we'll come back to the Sweet Centre again, me and Him. We might even come with my wife. And maybe my wife and my child, his grandchild.

And when we do come back we'll be different. The aroma will be the same, the Sweet Centre will continue to change, just like us, but the aroma will be the same.

The Homecoming

Lesley McEvoy

DOROTHY SAT ON THE low wall outside the impressive stone-built manor house she'd travelled so far to see. It was hard to imagine, here in this tranquil garden, covered in a pristine coating of early snow, that she was only a mile from the bustling City of Bradford.

Bolling Hall was the oldest building in Bradford, with parts of it dating back to medieval times. At least that's what her father had told her.

As a five-year-old, none of that had meant anything to her. All she'd cared about then, as she'd sat on his knee in these same gardens, was that they were together.

Precious father and daughter time, when her mother worked weekends and her father had taken her on special 'outings'. Stately homes and churches, had been the backdrop to their adventures. He'd known all about buildings being an architect, and she'd loved listening to him speak so passionately about mullioned windows and flying buttresses.

The manor house was a museum now. Had it been then, when her father brought her here, all those years ago?

'Must have been.' She murmured to herself, as she gazed

at the honey-coloured stone tower.

'Must have been what?' A quiet voice, made her jump.

'Sorry.' She smiled at the woman sitting on the wall beside her. 'I didn't see you there.'

The woman stared straight ahead. Her face in profile, chin buried into the folds of a shapeless cream, wrap-around coat – hair covered by a thick, woollen scarf – bundled up against the cold.

Dorothy waited for her to say something – but she didn't. Just sat – staring across the whitened lawn.

'I'm Dorothy, by the way.' She smiled.

The woman – whose age she couldn't quite determine – simply nodded.

'I was wondering whether Bolling Hall had been a museum, when my father brought me here, as a little girl?'

'You're not from these parts?' So softly spoken, that Dorothy had to lean forward to catch the words.

'Oh,' she laughed. 'My accent? Well, I was actually born in Bradford. My parents were too. But we went to live in America, when I was little. Dad got a job over there. I guess I sound more American than Yorkshire now.'

The woman nodded, pursing her lips thoughtfully. 'You've come back.'

It wasn't really a question, but Dorothy found herself answering it anyway.

'Only for a visit.' She glanced at the cardboard bag on the floor between her feet. When the undertaker handed it to her, she thought it looked like an oversized bottle bag.

'My dad never really settled in America. But Mom loved it, so he stayed for her.'

'That's love.' The woman's words were almost a whisper.

Dorothy nodded, feeling the unexpected sting of tears beneath her eyelids. If she blinked, they'd spill down her cheeks – so she sniffed them back – taking a deep lungful of crisp air. She didn't want to cry in front of a stranger. But at the same time, there was something comforting about talking to this quiet woman, who'd come to sit beside her.

'Mom passed away five years ago.' Dorothy fished a tissue out of her coat pocket and blew her nose. 'Dad said he wanted to come home.' She tipped her head back, looking at the dark fingers of frozen tree branches overhead.

'Even after all those years – he never felt at home in the States. Said his heart had always been here – in Yorkshire.'

'Aye.' The woman said, nodding slowly. 'This place gets you like that. Takes hold of something in your heart and doesn't let go.'

'Dad said he *needed* to come back.'

Dorothy half-smiled at the memory of the conversations they'd had – long into the night. Her trying to persuade him to stay and him – so determined that he had to return.

'Not just wanted to come back – *needed* to.'

'I know…'

Dorothy looked at her companion, as the woman's words trailed off, seemingly lost in a distant memory of her own.

'So, I helped Dad move back. Found him a little bungalow – not far from where I was born, in Wibsey. Do you know it?'

'Know all of this village.'

Dorothy smiled at that.

'Locals call where I live, 'The Village'. Greenwich Village, in Lower Manhattan. I guess even the biggest City can feel like that, if you know it well. Have you lived here long?'

'Forever, lass… forever.'

Dorothy looked at the bag between her feet, containing the 'scattering tube'. Somehow, it seemed like an undignified object, to be holding someone so precious. A cardboard container. The sooner she could free him from it, the better.

'He passed away two weeks ago. That's why I came back. This was one of his favourite places. He asked me to scatter his ashes here. It seems kind of right.' She glanced at the woman by her side. Funeral Director said I might have to get permission… you know, to scatter him. But I don't know who to ask?'

'Ask me. This is my house… my garden, now.'

'It's owned by the Council, isn't it?'

'No one owns the trees… the grass… the soil.' The woman said gently. 'Them that says they do, haven't been the keepers for all the time I have. My family go back with Bolling Hall for generations. My family worked for William Bolling. I spent my whole working life here too.'

'So, after the Bollings sold it… when it became a museum, you carried on working here?' Dorothy smiled. 'I like that. Following on a family tradition in the same place. What did you do here?'

'I kept its story.'

'A tour guide?'

The woman didn't reply. Lost in thought.

'Dad told me about this place, when I was a kid, but it was so long ago.' Dorothy took a packet of mints out of her pocket, offering one to the woman, who slowly shook her head. 'I do remember him saying, the house played a part in the English Civil War, though. He was a real military history buff.'

'Buff?'

'Fan… you know? Loved history, about wars and battles.'

'Bradford's fought many a battle, lass.'

Dorothy leaned forward, interested to learn more. After all, what were the chances of meeting someone who had worked here and knew so much about the place? Something fascinating to tell the family back home.

'Go on,' she encouraged.

'During the war between the king and parliament, Bradford was Puritan.'

'In support of Oliver Cromwell… parliament?' Dorothy said.

'Aye lass. Sir Thomas Fairfax, led our army. Earl of

Newcastle was for the King.'

'The Royalists?' Dorothy was warming to the story.

'Aye. They had far more men on foot and horse and surrounded the town. We had no hope of help from any place.' The woman slowly shook her head as she spoke, as if replaying it in her mind.

Dorothy listened. Enthralled by the way the woman told the story. As if they were living it now. Giving her a real sense of the place. Bringing everything to life in amazing detail.

'The Earl of Newcastle made his camp here, at Bolling Hall. The Royalists set their cannons on the hill, overlooking the town. The guns rained down upon the people, all through the night.'

'How awful,' Dorothy whispered.

'During the night, our men used the last of the powder and shot. There wasn't even a match left for their muskets.'

'What did Fairfax do?'

'In the early dawn, Fairfax fled and left the town to its fate.'

'He ran away?' Dorothy gasped.

'Newcastle. Knowing he had the town on its knees, retired to bed… here at Bolling Hall. The people, left in Bradford were very afraid of what was to become of them, because Newcastle had given orders, that in the morning, the town's people were to be put to the sword.

'What? You mean…?'

'Aye lass. Wiped out. Every last one.'

'No – what happened?'

'During the night, the Earl was woken from his sleep, by a lady, pulling the bedcovers away.'

'Who was she?' Dorothy asked, captivated.

Her companion shrugged. 'Some say a servant girl, who worked here. But Newcastle believed he'd seen a ghost – that she was a phantom. She beseeched him… "*Pity poor Bradford*".'

'Really?'

'He was so afraid, that in the morning he withdrew his order and the people of our town, were spared.'

'Wow.'

'After the siege, with loss of food and the people weakened, a pestilence befell Bradford. It took a hundred years for the place to recover.'

Dorothy took a long breath. 'This city has had its fair share of battles, then, as you say.'

The woman nodded slowly. 'But we're still here, lass. Stronger than ever. Our people have resilience… grit.'

Dorothy studied the woman's face – still in profile, as it had been the whole time. Making it hard to gauge her expression. But Dorothy knew, without seeing, that there were tears in the woman's eyes, just recounting a story. Moved to tears by the love she obviously had for her birthplace.

Dorothy wanted to reach out and touch the woman's pale hand, but didn't want to seem too familiar.

'It's not "poor Bradford" now though, is it?' she said cheerfully, trying to lighten the mood. 'Just look… it's become the City of Culture. My dad was so proud of that.'

'Rightly so, lass.'

Finally, the woman stood. She was smaller than Dorothy expected and for some reason, seemed older than she'd first thought. Her slight frame bundled beneath the pale woollen shawl-like coat.

She pointed to the trees on their right.

'Put your father to rest there, girl,' she said, quietly. 'It's beautiful in the summer and tranquil now, in winter. A good spot.'

Dorothy picked up the bag and walked over to the stand of trees. Stepping over the short wall onto the snow-covered lawn. Her boots crunched on the frozen earth underfoot, scattering ice crystals, like fallen diamonds.

She took out the cardboard tube and hugged it to her for a few minutes more, whispering final words to her father.

THE HOMECOMING

Dorothy could feel, rather than see the old woman behind her, watching the proceedings in silence.

'I've worked myself up to this moment for weeks,' Dorothy said. 'But now it's here... I don't want to let him go.'

'He'll always be with you, lass.' She heard the old woman saying – seemingly nearer to her shoulder than she thought. She could feel the reassuring presence at her back.

'I feel like I'm leaving him behind,' Dorothy sniffed, failing to stop the tears that slipped down her cold cheeks, in a warm trickle.

'I'm going to get on a plane tomorrow and fly thousands of miles away from here.' She squeezed the cardboard tube harder – in what felt like a final embrace. 'He'll be all alone.'

'He'll never be alone, lass,' the tender voice whispered over her shoulder. 'I'll be here.'

Dorothy half-turned, speaking over her shoulder. 'Will you come and visit him for me?'

'I'm here every day, lass,' came the reassuring reply. 'I'll watch over him.'

Dorothy opened the tube, stepping back, she held her arms out in front of her and gently shook the ashes out of the box, beneath the trees.

The grey powder fell softly onto the snow, settling on the glittering tufts of grass. A gentle breeze suddenly drifted across the garden, although there had been no wind until then. It lifted the fallen ash and carried it away from Dorothy, across the lawn, around the trunks of the other trees, until it seemed to dissolve in the freezing air.

Dorothy watched, until it all disappeared. Or perhaps it was the tears, welling up, to blur her vision.

'You're back home now, Dad,' she said softly, the words catching in her throat.

'Bradford looks after all of its children.' The old woman's voice behind her was receding.

Dorothy turned around, clutching the empty tube. Her companion was walking silently away, towards the Hall.

She followed her and as the woman reached the door, Dorothy paused for a moment, wiping her eyes with a tissue and blowing her nose. Composing herself before going inside.

She wanted to thank the old lady for her kindness. For sitting with a stranger and giving her comfort. Helping her through one of the toughest of days. Carrying out her father's last wish: to be laid to rest in the place they'd shared all those years ago.

A spot, in a child's mind, filled with magic and adventure. A place brought to life by her father's passion for the history of the building and its architecture – and now, by another miracle. On the day she'd come here to fulfil her final promise to him, she'd found possibly one of the few people who could add so much more to those memories. Enriching her father's stories to give her lasting, beautiful reflections on what could have been such a depressing day.

She hadn't heard the door to the hall close, but when she looked up, the old woman had gone inside.

Dorothy hurried over to the Hall, pushing open the double wooden door to step inside the welcoming warmth.

What had once been the entrance hall to the Manor house, was now a tiny gift shop. The young girl sitting at the desk, looked up and smiled as Dorothy entered.

'Morning,' the girl said brightly.

Dorothy looked beyond her into the Manor house kitchen in the next room.

'I'm looking for the lady who just came in,' she said, glancing around the display cabinets.

'Sorry?' the girl said, frowning.

'The woman, in the woollen wrap and headscarf… she came in just now. You must have seen her?'

'No one's been in all morning.'

'But I watched her come through the door, just now.'

THE HOMECOMING

The young girl shook her head, her smile firmly fixed, though she was starting to look confused.

'No. Sorry. I've been here the whole time. You're the first person in here today.'

Dorothy turned to look back at the door, as if she expected the woman to be standing there, laughing at them both.

'I don't understand,' she said, almost to herself.

'When I came to put the sign out, you were standing under the trees,' the girl said. 'You were talking to yourself.' She tilted her head sympathetically. 'I thought you were praying or something.'

'No,' Dorothy frowned. 'I was talking to her… to the old woman.'

The girl was starting to look uncomfortable. 'I only saw you… sorry.'

'You must have seen her. She was right behind me.'

The shop assistant just shook her head. Not knowing quite what to say.

'She said she was a tour guide here.' Something niggled at the back of her mind as she said that.

Had the woman actually *said* she was a tour guide? Or had Dorothy simply assumed it?

'We don't have formal tour guides,' the girl said. 'At least not in the time I've been here.' She got up from her chair and walked round the desk. 'On certain days, we have volunteers, who dress in period costume and tell visitors about the history of the Hall, though.'

'Yes.' Dorothy said, glad they'd finally cleared up the mystery. 'That would be her, then. She must be one of those. Come to think of it, her clothes were a bit old-fashioned. She said she was here every day.'

But the girl was already shaking her head. 'There are no volunteers here today,' she said. 'Just me.'

'How long have you worked here?' Dorothy wasn't about

to let it go. This member of staff must be new.

'Years... why?'

Dorothy persisted. 'She said her family had worked for William Bolling... before he sold the place to the council and it became a museum.'

The girl stood up and backed around the desk, putting the chair between them. Her expression cautious now.

'Err... I think you're mistaken.'

'No mistake.' Dorothy's tone was certain.

'The Bolling family haven't owned the Hall since the fifteenth century, when the Tempests took over. William Bolling died in 1316.'

Dorothy opened her mouth to say something... then closed it again, looking like a confused goldfish.

'It's been a museum since the First World War.' The girl continued, looking as though she'd rather be anywhere else, than having this conversation, with a deluded American woman.

'I'm sorry,' Dorothy mumbled, fumbling with the heavy door to stumble back outside into the ice-cold air, feeling slightly disoriented.

She stood on the Yorkshire stone slabs outside the Hall, taking deep lungfuls of air to clear her head.

She should have felt confused... or even afraid, but for some reason, she didn't.

As she stood there, alone, outside the Great Hall, a feeling of calm descended, wrapping around her shoulders like a warm blanket.

Everything became suddenly clear.

She would never be able to explain this to anyone back home, of course. But then, she didn't have to. It was enough that she understood who she'd met, on the day she'd needed to the most.

As if on cue, a breath of wind blew through the garden, lifting the stark, frozen branches of the trees – carrying the old woman's words to her again. Bringing with them a sense of calm. Of knowing.

'I'll watch over him…'

'Of course you will,' Dorothy said under her breath. 'Just as you watched over your village of Bradford, during the great siege.'

Before she left, Dorothy glanced back, one final time, towards the trees standing sentinel over her father's remains.

The sight of those stalwart custodians, giving her comfort. Certain now, that her father would be kept safe, in the arms of his beloved City.

The Ends

M. Y. Alam

IT'S LATE BUT STILL light on one of those rare, hot Sundays that end too soon. Should be a good day for a drive. Roads quiet, pace relaxed, drama absent.

In the car, a man on the radio speaks of news. I hear tell of a report about declining mental health, the young being susceptible to risk, vulnerable. A fragile teenager, name of Damien, is convinced his mental health is suffering. The boy has anxieties. Everything is so hard and no one understands what it's like to be him. After the news, the announcer introduces a play about an American living in London. Radio silence is better.

The roads aren't like I remember them. That easy vibe a thing of the past. Sundays were for cruising but these streets are now blocked with bollards or calmed with slabs of concrete and mounds of tarmac. Speed bumps committing a violence all their own, brutalising and mass murdering whole cars. Collective punishment or collateral damage, either way there's a cost.

*

My brother's first car, a rusty and falling apart 1973 Hillman

Avenger, we dubbed *The PYG* on account of the registration reading PYG 710K. The doors didn't lock and a screwdriver turned the ignition. Not exactly keyless entry and start. The PYG wore four different wheels and the boot flung open whenever it caught a pothole. With the suspension on the brink of collapse, the tyres scraped against wheel arches constantly, regardless of speed. The middle part of the exhaust disintegrated, the engine looser than a cheap whore discounting Friday-night-nasties, the PYG sounded like a tractor, spending more time on a ramp than it did on the road, with one mechanic after the other calling it 'a piece of shit', 'a deathtrap' or just plain 'embarrassing'.

Finished in various shades of aerosol white, today it might pass for a 'modified' vehicle but the PYG hadn't been roadworthy for years. With some coaxing, it would start up and we'd chip in toward fuel, staying on the road for hours, my brother manoeuvring that old shit-box all over and beyond this city.

*

It's still fertile, loaded with seedlings taking root, reaching for the sun, but this is not the same place I left. I navigate from one end to the other without thought but neither road nor city is mine any more. I've been back a year, and I'm still a visitor. No. Scratch that. I'm worse. A damned tourist, no less.

I'm heading over to Mad Mike's place. Him and me, we worked some jobs when we started out. Our employer, a man of usury, had us do his collecting. Dirty work. Mike enjoyed the action but it didn't sit right with me. A few months in, I'd had enough and moved to a different city with its own way of being. No time at all, landed myself in the business of finding instead of hurting people. I got good at it, building a reputation. Reliable. Steady. Efficient. You needed someone found, you found me first. People would have me locate their missing husband, wife, son, daughter, friend, whoever. No rock stars in that line of work, but word travelled back here. There's a grapevine.

Last time I saw Mad Mike, twenty and some years ago, I'd come back to do a job after his boss reached out and told me, all Don Corleone like, he'd consider it a favour. His daughter: gone a fortnight. No word, no warning. The loan shark father insulted, betrayed and furious, his depressed trophy wife drinking herself silly. Mike tearing the city inside out but getting nowhere.

Within a week, I find the daughter and her boyfriend, star-crossed lovers, holed up over Morley ways, out of their heads on who knows what. She wasn't much younger than us but the shit in her veins had easily put a decade on her. She went wild, clawing, kicking and screaming like a thing possessed. I got scratched up some, but Mike received countless licks to the face, a few kicks in the balls. He just stood there, like a dummy, taking it all. With her being the boss man's daughter, not like Mike could actually risk hurting her.

Never saw the boyfriend after that. I never spoke on it, either but his absence had Mike's dirty claws all over it. Now and then, finding them is no different to hurting them. There's a reason people want to stay unfound but you never know until the end, once you've put it all together. At that point, you either walk away or you set yourself the task of undoing the fuckery you've made.

Three Fridays ago, a chance encounter with Mike in what they call an ethnic food store. Took me a fast minute to clock his mug, half of which he'd covered with a long, but well-kept beard. Not a hipster beard and not one of those kept in check through regular barbering. He looked well, still fit and active. Mellowed, now, though. Calm. Relaxed, even.

Time was, Mike had a temper. Anger issues, you'd call it, now. Probably needed therapy of some kind but not an option back then. No. You kept it inside, pretended it didn't exist and you soldiered on. No complaining, no whining. Besides, he was Mad Mike and that meant something. One time, I saw him go toe to toe with a half dozen up-and-comers, hired because they were young, talked fast and looked the part. These men – kids, really – were clueless about what men like Mike could do.

Wednesday night, three in the morning, club car park over Batley ends. We get out of Mike's battered old Mondeo, they exit their high-end Merc in sync, like they'd been rehearsing this little move for months. Each one a copy of the other. Long leather coat, black jeans, big shiny boots, ponytail, studded gloves and, best of all, wraparound sunglasses. I figure them posers, well-heeled goths or sci-fi vampire hunters. Hollywood tough guys, complete with the moody dispositions and the dramatic back stories. Mike eyes their tools. Pool cues, baseball bats, one with a bike chain, another ready with the nunchucks, playing at Bruce Lee. The red mist falls, his breathing barely controlled, veins ready to burst, Mike's forehead wet with the sweat of anticipation. Without looking my way and before I can make a move, he tells me to back off and he's on them. Whole thing doesn't last more than a couple of minutes. The funny thing is, a stern talking to and a slap on the wrist would have done the trick just as well but Mad Mike, well, he had a name to live up to and, like I said, he enjoyed it. Doing violence, I mean.

Mike seemed out of place in the shop, his fingers fumbling sticks of okra into a bag, me dwelling on bitter melon. I take my time in these places, inspecting the things I've not touched often enough. Dhaniya, mooli, bengan, neelee murch, karela, bhindi, the stuff of sustenance for some. Occasionally it's for the likes of me, when we need reminding of the fragrances, colours and textures that made us who we once were, and might still be, if only in passing.

I looked at Mike. I could see him working through his

memory, the gears turning in his head. He said my name, moved closer and shook my hand before embracing the crap out of me. We made small talk, asking questions of little value, each of us performing the *long-time-no-see-good-to-see-you-you're-looking-well* dance. The gaps in our connection, all too present. Time had passed, the world had moved on, we'd changed. Nothing stands still. Mike was genuine about it though, maybe even pleased about seeing me. We agreed to stay in touch, exchanging numbers, the way people do when they prefer not to commit, to remain polite.

He called the next day. More small talk. I figured him retired and lonely but no, the man had a need. I offered a vague and non-committal response. He dropped me a text saying he needed a favour, signing off with a few smiley faces. A day later, more messages, becoming insistent. Sounded desperate.

*

I head onto Marlborough Road. Years ago, I had an accident on this very road, by the traffic lights at the bottom. It was late, the weather dry, visibility good. Nothing major, though. No real harm done, but the car was a goner. Another Corolla for the crusher.

I hit a right onto Manningham Lane. Grand old houses with bay windows, oversize front doors and smooth cut stone facades. Named Villas, or presenting themselves in Crescents and Squares, reserved for the daddies who ran this city a hundred and some years ago. Today's big shots prefer their own bubbles, outside the city, disinclined to eat the shit they serve everyone else. Say what you like about those rich Victorians, but at least they had the decency to commit to place. Hell, some of them even made the place their home.

For those toiling in the mills, the accommodation was modest, making their lives in the back-to-backs that are everywhere in this neck of the woods. Used to be a mill down the bottom of Clifton Street. Not been a mill for decades. Probably office space, or apartments, now.

Further along, shops and garages, cafés, a chippy, a dessert parlour and fast food joints selling the sweet taste of heart disease, diabetes and obesity. On the other side of the road, a carpet shop, a plumber's merchant, a furniture warehouse, a couple of barbering joints. One's named itself 'studio' and the other 'lab'. These boys, they don't just cut hair, they research and develop it, like you would a new drug. The lab has a red, blue and white barber's pole above the door. Inside, old meets and fucks with the new. There'll be a vintage bicycle hanging off the ceiling while the latest in LED lighting technology illuminates the room. Meanwhile, two or three hair technicians in too-tight trousers, skin-tight shirts and gold nooses around their necks will spend their days chatting shit to their customers, gliding around the retro barbering chairs, snipping, clipping and fussing over their prey. When business is quiet, they'll busy themselves restocking their shelves with gels, creams, potions and lotions. Mostly they'll earn their coin trimming beards and neatening hairlines of the young and the fashionable who have their own routines and rituals. Beard trimmed weekly, hair cut fortnightly, eyebrows shaped monthly. Yes, even men do that shit now.

*

Mullaney, an Irishman who looked old enough to have done some blood-letting and minor surgical work in his day, must have learnt his trade shearing or butchering sheep. He wore thick-lensed glasses, his hands in a constant state of tremble, chain-smoking Player's Navy Cut fags. A quid for a haircut and, aside from the condoms, Brylcreem and razorblades, Mullaney offered nothing else. Not even conversation. Mullaney was a bad bet to begin with, but the thing is, he was

Jimmy Mullaney and not Bhatti, Ghani or Fazal. And that meant everything.

Uncle Fazal, an old army friend of my dad, didn't say much unless you were of his generation. A part-time barber, he operated from home. He was quick, efficient and consistent. You'd go in, he'd seat you on a wooden chair in the middle of the living room, tie a nylon sheet around your neck and get busy with his scissors, comb and manual clippers. Short, back and sides, a cut he'd mastered decades ago. All the while, his family sat there, carrying on as if him cutting someone's hair in their home was normal, no big deal.

Uncle Ghani, a ten-minute walk away, was a nice, friendly old man who wore a prayer cap and sported a closely trimmed beard. He had a shop, his sons helping out in the business of clipping, cutting and occasionally cut-throat shaving. He didn't say much to people like me, either. We didn't have much in common. Not like we could compare notes on the latest song by The Specials, or whether white socks were really that cool.

Uncle Bhatti, the busiest of the three, had a shop up the road, on the same row as the Post Office, a bank and Khan's the grocer and butcher. Mirrors on the wall, sink basins in the counter. Pride of place, two leather chairs that moved up and down by a foot-operated lever. There were always a few old men in, chewing the fat, reading Urdu newspapers, smoking fags, coughing their guts out. A ghetto blaster on a shelf, blaring out C90 tapes of Pothwaari Shaher, while the barber and his guests passed judgement on the wisdom they heard, digging into the meaning of it all, moving their heads around, eyes closed, practising devotion in a state of near trance.

Crudely taped to the windows and walls, pictures of male models sporting modern looks and smiles. You would go in, point to the style you wanted and Uncle Bhatti would look at you, then look at his chair. You'd sit, he'd tie the sheet around you, and then grip your tiny, insignificant head and let the clippers do their work. Two minutes later, you'd leave his shop in tears.

So, you discovered Mullaney, and believed he had to be better than any of those operators. Trouble is, he was probably the worst of the bunch. Like Uncle Bhatti, he had images of how wonderful and fashionable hair could be, but Mullaney's framed pictures added a touch of class to the operation. A quiffed, flicked, feathered, layered and precise head of hair you aspired to and politely requested. What you got was a crew cut at best, but if he caught you in one of his coughing fits, you'd exit with a lopsided, uneven lawnmower job, looking worse than a punk rocker. That old butcher even managed to cut my ear once. On the bright side, he gave me a plaster. Like I said, class.

*

At the turning just before the filling station, a fancy-looking ride pulls out onto the main road, waiting for someone to give way. The window rolls down, revealing a driver barely out of his teens. This kid is not fragile, anxious or vulnerable. Yellow draped around his neck, more precious metal dripping off a wrist which rests casually on the steering wheel. He's wearing knock off Ray-Bans, a beard, a smile. Pleased with himself, he nods in time to the vibrations bursting out of his car, colliding with every surface they meet. It's German and red, his car. Clean. Polished. Laboured over, loved but altered – the wheels, the paint, the glass. I slow down, peer down the road and see the commotion caused by lots of cars and even more people. I flash my headlights, and the kid offers me a thumbs up as he joins Manningham Lane. His smile still genuine, growing wider as he floors the pedal, the tyres squealing, leaving streaks of black on the tarmac and a trail of blue in the air.

I hook a left and crawl down the road. I find a spot and pull up by a car park, a venue for some kind of car enthusiast get-together. They're more than enthusiasts, somehow. Engines are being thrashed but out of this chaos, there is order, a harmony of sorts. Screaming exhausts, only pausing to take breath and then, as if protesting, they explode. Louder than a gun, some with more depth than canon fire. The crowd shows appreciation by making its own din of whoops, whistles and yays. It's not a car park, and these are not cars. It's a damned concert hall and these are instruments, an orchestra creating music unlike any other.

The human traffic is mostly young, only here to show off their machines. Regardless of their background, they're all wearing the same kind of garb, sportswear and designer labels preferred over anything else. Tracksuits, trainers, short haircuts for the lads, longer and straighter strands for the lasses, a few favouring the application of thick marker pen over their eyebrows for some reason.

*

Where the car park stands, a stone's throw from the football ground, was once a street, the place I first called home. Next door to us lived the Whites. Head of the family, old timer name of Frank, worked the ground at Valley Parade, keeping the turf alive. His wife was Anne, but my mother insisted we call her Mrs White. Mrs White knew me since birth. She'd remind me, with high-pitched affection, that she would hold and comfort me during regular bouts of colic during my infancy. I didn't know what it was, but the way she talked, it was as if colic produced gold eggs or some other such treasure.

Mrs White looked older than her years but radiated a joy for life with a toothless smile and ever open arms. She would tell my mother that new people meant new friends and new friends meant a new life, or at least a new way of living. Silver-grey shoulder-length hair, clipped back at the front, Mrs White spent most of her time either scrubbing at the front doorstep or washing clothes and hanging them out to dry on the line that stretched from our side of the street to the other.

When not attending to chores, she favoured singers, having grown a soft spot for Nat King Cole and Ella Fitzgerald which Danny, the Whites' son, barely tolerated. In their front room, they had a stereogram housing a record player, a radio and built in speakers. Bought the thing brand new from Woods Music Shop, down the road, proud to have paid for it with the cash she'd been saving for years.

★

I linger between a Ford and a Honda, both screaming for attention. At some point in their lives, their skins might have been white, or blue or some other shade that registers as colour to the human eye. Now they are finished in tones concocted and layered on by a lunatic who, in another world, would be exhibiting his work in galleries, museums, and celebrated as a loved but flawed genius. The Honda is white, inflected with gold, and maybe some pink. Hints of blue. Or green. Red. No, not red. Purple. Maybe purple. These cars, they must mean something. Maybe they even speak, through some code, or signals and clues. Must be a language in there somewhere but I can't hear or speak it. Even madness can fashion beauty. Trouble is, only the insane can see it.

I walk around some more but my head hurts. Not for me, this noise. These people, hell bent on deafening themselves and anyone who happens to be close by, they're still young, not realising everything has a price. For now, their lives are brimming with potential, despite the world being against them. They're either oblivious or deluded. Then again, could be they are happy in their ignorance. No, not ignorance. Optimism. They can do anything, be anyone and go anywhere. At least they've got that. For now, reality is for the likes of their fathers and their mothers.

THE ENDS

★

My mother enjoyed Mrs White's lengthy contemplations on the weather, the price of fish and her memories of the war she experienced as a child. In no time at all, sharing stories became ordinary, both telling each other tales of adversity, and of moments which created laughter. Soon, sharing food became a custom, too. My mother would cook, make a few plates, and I would distribute to a handful of neighbours who would return the plates filled with their own cooking. It wasn't exactly a give and take, more like a courtesy. On a typical day, we had maybe four or five extra dishes to enjoy. Well, not always enjoy. I mean, some of the neighbours, try as they might, they couldn't cook for shit.

Mrs White embraced and savoured the flavours that were until then alien to her tongue. Garlic, ginger, chilli, turmeric, paprika and fenugreek brought her palate joy which she would communicate with passionate shrieks and accidentally loud burps. As for desserts, she was a martyr to her diabetes but could never resist the sweet rice, halva or kheer.

Their son Danny scared the hell out of me. These days, I occasionally see him in a dream but that motherfucker traumatised me as a kid. Often, he'd give me a good kicking, punishment for existing, for being in his sight, and for having the nerve to trouble him in taking chase. Kids like me, we saw Danny, we ran.

The affection his mother had for me drove Danny mad. Danny didn't like much in the world to begin with, but for people like me he reserved a vicious passion. Considering himself a rebel, he smoked tipless cigarettes, sipped Double Diamond pale ale beer from a can, favouring a black leather jacket over a t-shirt, dirty jeans worn half mast, Dr. Martens' boots threaded with white laces. He had ink on his hands. The indigo stick man of The Saint seemed ironic, but the Yorkshire Rose, 'Mam' labelled underneath, spoke of something like love.

Most evenings, Danny and his mates would stand at the end of the street, necking beers, shooting the breeze. After a few cans, his tongue loosened, he would set about his preaching. *This is my city. It's where I'm from. This city is my city, our city. Outside here, there's nothing. This place, it's in our blood. If people ask, you say you're from here, from this city. This is our city, and no one's ever taking it away.*

A few cans later, his rhetoric would evolve. *Backbone of this country, this place. Not anymore, though. We've been betrayed by everyone, we have. The government, the employers, and even our own neighbours and family.* A few more swigs, the tempo would shift again. Like some fly-by-night street hawker, he would perform for his mates and anyone else in earshot. *Everywhere you turn, there's pakis, sambos, nignogs. Facts, plain and simple. They're taking everything.* Danny and his little gang would stick around, spitting variations of the same old verses, eventually wandering off, looking to release their pent-up anger on some poor sap. As long as it wasn't me, it didn't matter.

Frank was different. I liked Frank. No airs, no graces. A working man. Honest, decent and plain speaking. Not a fussy man, and not one to complain about his lot in life, the condition of the working classes or the state of the world. A flat cap perched at an angle on his balding head, a tweed blazer with holes at the elbows and polished black brogues on his feet. Frank sported no teeth at all, an unlit rolled up fag hanging from his lip, wobbling around in sync with occasional and short flurries of speech. Frank got on with most people, especially my dad. They'd sit and talk for hours, one explaining his own verse, and the lines of Ulama Iqbal, Mian Mohammad Baksh and Bulleh Shah, the other musing over the wisdom of Philip Larkin, Ted Hughes and Wilfred Owen.

Mrs White, she stayed in that house for the rest of her life, first with Frank and then alone. Danny became a door-to-door salesman, donning a cheap suit and flogging overpriced vacuum cleaners. He made decent money, convincing old-age pensioners and the like that his product would better their lonely and miserable lives. Soon enough, he was married, then fatherhood, then a routine. He'd work late every day, capping his evening off with a couple of pints down the local. Weekends he'd relax. Saturday meant washing the car in the drive, giving the lawn a trim, maybe some DIY followed a weekly shop at the supermarket, rounding off the night with a takeaway curry, a bottle of wine and cheap pop for the kid. Danny was a family man. Settled. Except he wasn't. He kept it low, but on Saturday nights, Danny and his mates let themselves loose: taxi drivers, shop keepers and later, women wearing headscarves.

I'd still visit Mrs White as I got older. The street had changed completely by then but that kept them going, Danny's mam and mine. New people, new friends, new life.

*

Mike lives close to the car park, him favouring these ends more than most. Our former boss, the money lender, hated it here. First chance he got, he went suburban, to a neighbourhood not tainted as deprived or damaged. Landscaped gardens, a fleet of cars in his garage, a games room, a bathroom at every turn. No use to him now, any of that. Within days of his daughter's return, someone put the hurt on him but botched the job, leaving him in ICU for months. ICU. No cure for that kind of damage. Rumour was his daughter, heartbroken as she was, put out the paper but she didn't have that kind of scratch or the contacts. Could have been any one of the hundreds her father had screwed into a life of debt, financial or otherwise. Given the right motivation, some might have done it for free. Makes no odds. He's as good as dead. Slowly rotting away, spending his days laid up, breathing, eating and shitting through pipes.

Mike occupies a rented two-up, two-down. Take one step out of the front door and you're on the pavement. Might not be landscaped but it's a garden, of sorts. There is a doorbell but I knock and then knock again. The door opens and he stands before me, showing the beginnings of a smile.

'It works,' he says, pressing the doorbell.

'So it does.'

'Come in, it's alright, come in. Won't bite, promise.'

It's sparse, on account of the room's dimensions. Clean, well-kept and furniture a touch above Ikea. Not that Ikea's bad, but self-assembly gear can only be so good. The fully-tiled fireplace is what they call an original feature. It throws me back to my childhood, when I learnt to keep fire fed with coal, raking and extending its life during the day, sweeping and binning the dead ashes every morning.

Mike makes tea and sits opposite me on a chair, insisting I take the sofa. There is only a wooden coffee table between us. That, and the years.

'I'm really glad you came,' he says, his accent thick, a reminder of the one I lost.

'Yeah.'

'Nice,' he resumes. 'Were good seeing you. You know, been a while, like.'

I was right. He's not the same man I knew. No anger, now. Could be he's cured himself, but someone like Mad Mike doesn't get so damned chipper without some kind of intervention. Could be drugs or maybe the countless headfuck therapies they offer you now. Thing of it is, I'm pleased for him.

'So,' I say, edging closer. 'A favour.'

On the fireplace, a photo frame. A man, a woman and a child. The woman looks familiar but I can't place her. I've seen her, maybe even know her but it's not coming to me.

'You okay?'

I can't stop myself from looking at the photo and I don't know why.

'Yeah, sure, Mike.'

Mike, his wife and their daughter, an image fixed half a decade in the past at least. Never figured Mike as the marrying type, or the settling down and having a kid type. The mother, she's smiling but only for the lens, for the world. The daughter is five or maybe six years old. Her head nestles under Mike's chin, her arms around his neck, holding on to him the way daughters cling to their fathers. I had a photo like that, somewhere. For the life of me, I can't remember where it is.

Mike is happy because he's hopeful. Not drugs or therapy after all. Having a kid, it changes everything, gives your life meaning, makes you whole. Until one day, she's not there and there's not a damned thing you or anyone else can do about it. Having a kid, it fucks you up differently.

'You're looking really well, mind you,' he says. 'How've you been?'

'Like I said, I'm here. So,' I pause, growing weary of this civility. 'What is it, Mike?'

This, the expression he wears is the one I remember. Mad Mike is back. Serious, angry, veins showing on his forehead, ready for some violence. But no, it's not that. The man is troubled. There's a difference.

'It's important,' he begins, calming the situation with outstretched hands, that frown turned upside down, for now. 'It's important that you do this for me. I can pay.'

The penny drops. I know why I'm here. There's no trace of them, other than the fireplace photograph. Either they're dead or they're gone. Mike doesn't need to speak on it but he does.

Was a time when I thought there's nothing sorrier than seeing a grown man cry. A man who cries isn't much of a man. It goes against a man's nature. But seeing a man called Mad Mike in despair has a quality all its own.

Sobbing followed by breath being held. An attempt to control, to stop this expulsion of emotion. Exhaling with a shriek, the leaking of sound, held back before it becomes something else. Mike is subduing. This must stop. He must control himself. This is not him, and not what he does. A deep breath in, then a slow but uneasy, juddering and unsteady release. He's trying. God loves a trier. Trying but struggling. Struggling and failing. The second he gains some composure, it starts again. Involuntary. Telling, urging and begging himself to stop being such a bitch. Such a fucking pussy, crying like this. Stop being such a bitch pussy. He's still there, pushing the thing down inside of him, suppressing it, whatever it is, this composition of pain, grief and guilt.

If you've been there, you know it's best to work through it on your own even though it doesn't get any better, any easier. It's always there. You squeeze it, you wring it and you make it small. You put it in a box, and you swallow that box and you push it down, into the darkness. A dark thing belongs in a dark place. You taste it and you feel it as it moves down your throat, through your gullet, deep into your gut. Deeper, into the deepest part of you. So far deep that you want it to come out. You want to shit it out so it's no longer in you. So it's gone. So finally, it's gone, evacuated, and maybe even lost forever. But the fucking thing doesn't come out. It just stays in there. Now and then you feel it bubbling back up, resurfacing and bringing the darkness with it, and you start all over. You push it down again, hoping this time it'll work and this time it'll go but it never does. You realise it's no longer in a box. The thing of it, the substance and the mass and the form of it, it's leaked out and infected every part of you, now. You've absorbed it. It's in your blood, your lungs, and worst of all, it's in your head and it's there for good.

In between all the sobbing and whining, he offers up the ask. Takes a while, him puking guilt, pain and remorse all over me. All the while, I can't look at him. I stare at the photograph on the fireplace, hoping it comes to life and tells me what to do. Doesn't have to, though. Like I said, there's a reason some people don't want to be found.

*

I drive back onto Manningham Lane, heading homeward but as I continue, I scan the roads and streets I left. They're still in me, somewhere. Here, it's where I'm from. Outside this city, nothing exists. This place, it's in my blood. When people ask, I say I'm from here, from this city. This is my city, and no one can ever take it away.

I drive through Girlington, and on to Ingleby Road. The old Allied Colloids factory is no more, in its stead dull new houses built to last years, decades at a push. I find myself taking a right, then jumping across the give-way. Been a while since I last visited the people I might see in my sleep.

The sun's still out, it's warm and the graves are rich with flowers in bloom. People are visiting, offering prayers, speaking to and for their dead. Gravesites of the Victorian powerful look like entrances to tombs, grand, Yorkshire stone dressed as angels, crosses, scripture. More modest plots for those who sweated their lives away. All of them arranged in rows. We all hold the same station in death, but looking around here, you'd think otherwise.

One section devoted to me and mine is no longer big enough and so, we've started taking more land, more space. Must be hundreds, maybe thousands of us here now, each in a plot of their own. At some point, the space will run out and we'll have to find somewhere else to dig and bury. I remind myself I'll be here at some point.

Mrs White's headstone is simple, her grave overgrown with dandelions and weeds. I remember her face, and imagine her carrying me, soothing me as I struggle with whatever the hell colic is supposed to be. The thought of her makes me smile. She died in her sleep without any lingering illness. Not like her to become a burden. Danny, buried a few graves over from her, met his end weeks after his mum died. Victim of a hit and run on Marlborough Road. Tragic. It was in the paper. Middle of the night, the road dry, visibility good. On Danny's headstone, a crucifix and an inscription telling its own story: 'Loving father, husband, son. Resting'. Frank died before them both, but I can't find his piece of turf.

I go back to the graves in the Muslim section, approaching the childhood friends who've already gone, before locating and praying for my own blood. The headstones in various shapes, sizes and colours, featuring their name, place of birth, the span of their years. They all have religious scripture. Two have verses, each penned by the same poet, one for himself, the other for his wife.

The Hole in the Heart

Becky Cherriman

THE BRADFORD HOLE, WE called it, or The Hole in the Heart, a muddy wound left to fester for a decade in the centre of the city. It couldn't have been predicted and couldn't be helped, the developers said, given few people were in a position to invest after the crash.

I wasn't surprised that a sinkhole appeared in the world's finances. Like I used to say to our Paul when he'd have one too many pieces of Mother's Pride with Golden Syrup, greed doesn't fill anything; it just makes you hungrier. They call them fat cats for a reason, gorging on the cream of the workers, leaving the rest of us with skimmed down piss. Paul would roll his eyes when I said that. He was at that stage by then, donning his grammar school blazer like a cloak of superiority. Things were already souring between us. But you think it's normal, don't you, with teenagers? Rebellion. Not that he had much to rebel against, not with me.

It was years before they started digging. God knows what they were faffing around at. 'Give it back to the people' someone graffitied on the hoardings. You'd walk past statements like 'Good Times' while, behind, rats snacked on the dead tissue of Bradford, made a playground of the uncleared rubble.

And all for a shopping centre.

We saw didn't we, what happened in Sheffield with Meadowhall – shutting down the steelworks and building that oversized greenhouse packed with every chain you could name? Thatcher has a lot to answer for, including turning shopping into a national pastime. At least in Cas they got Xscape where you can have a laugh, shooting each other with laser guns and that.

Shops in the city centre had never been that busy anyway, even when I were a kid. Except for HMV. I used to go after school, flick through the cassettes then head to The Arndale Centre. Me and me mates would drape ourselves from the balcony and drool over the St Bede's boys. Sometimes literally. Like when Zee spit on this lad. She knew him from middle school, hated him because he'd tied her up with a skipping rope once and wouldn't let her go.

What was worse than the *proposed* shopping centre, was the gaping lack of it. No movement for years. Nowt. Just these big Westfield tombstones commemorating Bradford's fairy tale future while our real future lay beneath the rubble. Made me think of those sunken-in graves in Undercliffe Cemetery or Haworth – Zee reckoned the people inside were cursed.

We went to Haworth on this school trip once, learned about the Brontës. The tour guide told us rain fell into the graves at the top of the village, washed typhoid and cholera off the corpses and into the water system. So many children's graves. Stone carvings of angels and lambs, engravings like *In the Arms of Jesus*. The thought of kids dying because the rich don't think poor people deserve clean water makes me gip. Sometimes there are several to a tombstone – including two brothers called Joseph, one two years old, the other only one.

I went back there recently, got a proper fright when I noticed one of them was called Paul David. *Resting with the Angels.* Six-years-old. Our Paul was adorable at that age, building tracks around the living room and even up the skirting boards on the stairs. He'd recite all these facts about locomotives and spend hours counting the number of sleepers, make me be a tunnel by standing over the tracks or put my cup of tea near the train so it looked like steam was coming from the engine.

Anyway, on the school trip, we bumped into another group, kids from somewhere posh like Leeds or Harrogate. One of them asked where we were from, then said Bradford were a shithole. Mel threatened to smack him one and Zee nearly got caught flicking the vs. Luckily our teacher was distracted because theirs was quoting Heathcliff to her (English teachers really get off on that stuff). On the coach back, we did the usual chant, 'Where do you come from?' We come from Bratfud, shitty, shitty Bratfud.' It felt alright if it were us saying it, there were a pride in it.

But that hole. We didn't dig it.

No wonder that, by then, more and more young people were leaving the city to find better jobs. I was well happy when I saw the clutch of students handing out leaflets outside the Midland. One had a placard with a demolition ball and the words *Don't Wreck our Future!* The guy who gave me a leaflet was wearing a keffiyeh. They were part of the Occupy movement and inspired by the Arab Spring. *A New Dawn*, one headline proclaimed when the revolutions happened. Those students really believed we could knock it all to the ground, build something out of the detritus. That was why I had to be part of the protest, why I was one of them that broke into the site.

Not that I should call it breaking in. Legally speaking, technically even, it weren't because someone had a mate in the council who gave them a key. Even if we had, we knew the most the police would do would be to stick us in a cell overnight and give us an ASBO, or whatever they were calling it by then. Completely different scale in the Middle East. In Egypt, the police blinded revolutionaries with rubber bullets, chucked tear gas grenades into the underground, kidnapped young men, and locked them up. It took ages for their families to find out where they were. I kept thinking about Paul, how I'd feel knowing he was in a cell somewhere miles away, suspended from a metal grate by his arms or thumped with batons. Course Paul would never have been involved in anything like that. Too conformist. You just hope he wouldn't be holding a baton.

It was November 2011, not the best time of year to be camping out but I took a day of annual leave, lent a tent from Jan, and went along. There weren't many of us, but that cheer when we unlocked the gate and rushed through, it felt like we were a wave, following bigger waves and, that other, even bigger waves would come after us.

A lad wanted to borrow a couple of pegs – he'd lost some of his at Glastonbury. While we wrestled with guy ropes and canvas, we got chatting. Tommy, his name was. Couldn't have been much older than Paul. He reckoned the hole was embarrassing, a personal insult to every Bradfordian, that it implied we were missing something other people had. And he wasn't just talking shopping centres. Missing. 'Those s's make you think you should be quiet about it, ashamed somehow,' he said.

Everyone agreed – the hole was an eyesore, an insult to the people of Bradford. Even the police were kind of on our side. Well, if someone on the council gave you a key, they said, who are we to argue? People forget most police are working class. They have the same interests as the rest of us, at least in their personal lives. Plus, they needed to think about their public image after the riots. Defending an Australian retail company wasn't their battle.

There were political diehards at the occupation. Tattooed white blokes with dreads. Two lesbians with the double Venus in their ears. A few well-groomed Asian lads from Undercliffe. There was even a Spanish guy came over from Indignados.

Occupy wasn't about individuals though. It was about the masses, the 99 per cent. Us. It was about channelling all that hope and anger, taking the bowl away from the fat cats so the rest of us wouldn't have to shove one another out of the way while we scavenged for the scraps.

Another thing we all agreed on, we were sick of London getting everything.

I wasn't surprised when Paul told me they'd offered him an internship down there. He'd always done well at school then smashed it with a First in Economics. I was hoping uni would loosen him up a bit, stir him politically but he got more conservative if anything. As far as I know, he didn't even get laid. Not that he'd tell his mum, I suppose. But working for a bank! It was hardly how I'd brought him up. Still, I tried to be supportive. 'Congratulations. At least you won't be skint.' Part of me was relieved he wouldn't have to worry about how to pay the rent if he had to take a sick day.

'Like you, you mean?' He could be like that sometimes, Paul, a bit cruel.

I tried not to look up at the damp flowering on the wall, at the bane-of-my-existence kettle beneath that had made me exceed my overdraft limit a couple of years back. I was still in the red, still hadn't paid for the bloody kettle, only the interest. What us English will suffer for a cuppa, hey?

'I'll be out of your hair by the end of the month.'

'Don't say that Paul, I'll miss you terribly.'

'Mmmm,' he said.

Something prickled behind my eyes. Like grit. 'How often do you think you'll come home?'

He shrugged. 'I'll try to make it back for Christmas.'

December 1991. A small chubby index finger prods me awake. I open my eyes and am confronted by a far too close-up glittery beard. Five minutes later, Paul's dipping his nose in the stocking, hungry as a blooming reindeer. His face when he found the satsuma – pure delight!

Empty nest, they call it. When the young have flown or fallen.

Eggs and beans never tasted so good as they did cooked over flames that Friday of the occupation. The logs beneath charred and crumbled like a land hit by apocalypse. 'It's just so ugly what they're proposing,' an old man said, 'apathetic architecture.'

'Like giant Duplo bricks,' I agreed.

'It disrespects our history. All those Victorian buildings made when Bradford was the heart of the wool trade, when it beat out enough wool to winter clothe the empire.'

'Well, somewhere had to clothe them. They'd destroyed the textile industries in the Global South,' a young mixed heritage woman opposite sniped through the smoke, 'and most of the resources were nicked.'

My gaze fell on the blue threads in her braids. 'Good point.' Being inside those elegant buildings, staring up at their grand atriums and plaster cornices always makes me dizzy – it's not just the beauty, it's the palatial excess, the twisted history.

'Here,' Tommy nudged me, 'watch this.' He put on a fire glove and stuck his hands into the flames. Plucked out a shard of eggshell and dropped it in his beaker of water, held it up. 'What colour is it?'

I took it closer to the flame. 'Silver.' It's silver.

'How the fuck did you do that?' the woman with the blue braids asked.

Tommy shrugged then grinned so wide I could see the silver of his filling far back in his mouth. 'Alchemy.'

Paul did come back for Christmas – turned up with a 24-carat bracelet for me. Not really my sort of thing but it was a lovely thought. I cooked turkey and we watched *Wallace & Gromit* and *The Royle Family*. He even helped with the washing up. But on Boxing Day, he went out. Don't know who with – he were a bit cagey so it might have been a date. When he came back, he were raging, spouting stuff about lazy single mothers and benefits.

'Come on, Paul.'

'What?' His pupils were pinpoints of hate. 'Some of us work hard for what we've got.' A rented flat in Kensington. Hefty bonuses. 'By the way, I'll be leaving tomorrow. I've had enough of this shithole.'

'Can't you stay another day? I was thinking we might head to Richard Dunn, see if I've still got it in me to go on the slide.' He looked like I'd belted him. I didn't get it. 'You used to love going there, remember?'

'I'm not nine years old, Mother.' He stomped his way up the stairs, precisely like he did when he was nine.

I shouted after him. 'Being an adult doesn't have to mean a life without fun.'

The next morning, I watched through the window as he walked away, a snapshot of pain in his expression.

He stopped coming after that. The calls became less frequent too. I got the mega bus down a couple of times. But he would follow me round with a cloth and flip out about me leaving a cup on the worktop or slinging my clothes over the arm of the sofa bed. It felt like I was dirtying up his place just by being there. Not that he wanted to go into the city together either.

Carol Ann Duffy calls it the hidden grief when your children leave. It's the point of parenthood, isn't it? To get them ready to fly the nest. So why is it so painful? Whenever I suggested me coming down to London again, he'd make up some excuse – a work conference, dinner with his boss, extra work due to the crash. Our relationship straggled on a dry stalk. Sometimes we went three months without a conversation. I dreamt of searching the soil for lost pieces of China.

By the Saturday there were around 50 of us plus the papers. A middle-aged couple from Dublin, a few kids. George

Galloway rocked up, gave a bit of a speech. Not a huge fan to be honest, but at least he lived in Bradford, at least he had to walk past that fucking hole like the rest of us.

A couple of teenagers who'd heard about the occupation wandered in. 'I just wish they'd hurry up and build a Zara,' one of the lasses said. Her mate giggled and hushed her. But at least they could see that you don't have to put up with it, that people can get together and challenge injustice when it's on their doorstep.

It was a couple of weeks after the protest when he called.

'Paul?'

There was a gnawing silence. Then, 'Mum, can I come home?' If his name hadn't flashed up on the phone, I might not have known it was him, he sounded so different, so… flattened.

'Of course. Why? What's happened? Are you okay?'

'Not really.'

'Oh Paul.'

'I might need to stay for a while.'

'It's your home. Always. What's troubling you?'

'Nothing and everything.' His breath shuddered down the line. 'I'm just a bleak house.' Bleak house – our code for sadness when his friends refused to play with him, when he broke his leg and was struggling on crutches, my way of explaining a bad dose of PMT.

'We'll get you right,' I said.

'I know, Mum. Thanks.'

Westfield were pissed off about the publicity around the protest, said it was self-defeating, that we should have arranged to meet. But meetings don't change owt, do they, not unless you're the one holding the purse? And we reckon the protest nudged them into saying yes to the temporary urban garden. It lifted me to see green in the city centre and that mural was great, so lively. Still, it was two years before they started building.

On Bonfire Night 2015 The Broadway Shopping Centre finally opened. By late spring, I was ready to face my nemesis. I met Paul in one of the shopping centre cafés. He ordered a double espresso. I asked for an ordinary coffee, but the woman didn't know what that meant. He grinned and there was love in it. 'I think my mum wants a flat white.'

'Ta love,' I said. I stared up at the glass ceiling. 'Feels like we're in a spaceship.'

'I quite like it,' he said.

After we'd finished our drinks, we crossed the marble floor, our feet sliding across the natural notes of the white tiles, tapping occasionally on the black and headed for City Square.

It was balmy as owt, the first hot day of the year, and they'd turned on the fountain. We sat on one of the wooden benches near a man in a white kurta.

'You know,' Paul said, 'I was so proud of you for protesting about that bloody hole, I loved that Bradford wasn't taking it.'

I looked across the teeming Mirror Pool. A woman in a hijab and bare feet. Men without t-shirts drinking from cans. Teenagers in Crocs.

'In the city I was surrounded by colleagues in Armani suits, snorting coke off the back of their hands,' he said.

'I thought that was just a stereotype.'

'It's not all of them but yeah, it happens.'

Pink bikinis. Trunks. Floppy hats.

'My shares were building up thanks to a Christmas bonus that effectively came from taxpayer bailouts, and I just felt, you know, emptied out. Everywhere on the news there was the impact of austerity, especially in the North – people dying because they'd lost their benefits, children being pushed into poverty. And then I saw it in the paper, that image of the hole. It ate away at me. I knew if I stayed, there'd be nothing left of me in a year.'

So many kids scooping the liquid silver off the water. The whole of Bradford refracted. 'Well, *I'm* glad you came back.'

Two small, wet palms slapped at my thigh. 'Hello Darling.' I kissed Rehan's black hair, drew him in. 'Where's Mummy?' I asked. He broke out of the hug and my gaze followed his index finger to Amina who was walking toward us, forearms strained with the weight of her bags.

Rehan tugged at Paul's hand.

'You've been told,' I said to Paul. 'You'd best take off your trainers.'

Amina let the bags collapse onto the bench. One sock still on, Paul stood to greet her with a tender kiss on the cheek.

'Dad! Come on!'

Amina sat beside me and offered me one of the bananas that was poking over the top before peeling her own. We watched the two of them run off together as the pattern of the fountains changed, each beginning its arc toward a central point above us. Rainbows formed.

About the Contributors

Nick Ahad is an award-winning writer, broadcaster and journalist working across TV, theatre and radio. His TV work includes the BBC drama *Better* and several years writing for *Emmerdale*. He has written for the stage, including the acclaimed 2024 adaptation of Onjali Q. Rauf's *The Boy at the Back of the Class*, and for the radio, most notably *Partition*, which was broadcast on BBC radio stations across the country at midnight on 14 August, 2017, to mark 70 years of Indian independence. A radio presenter for over a decade, he has fronted the Nick Ahad Radio Show on BBC Radio Yorkshire and hosted Radio 4's *Front Row*.

M. Y. Alam is the author of three novels: *Annie Potts is Dead, Kilo,* and *Red Laal*. He has had several short stories published and is the editor of *Made in Bradford* and *The Invisible Village*, pioneering works of oral history. He is a researcher, lecturer and Head of Department at the University of Bradford.

Bill Broady was born in Leeds and educated in Bradford, York and London. A former croupier, cartographer and care worker, he has written four novels: *Swimmer* (HarperCollins, 2000), *Eternity is Temporary* (Portobello, 2006), *The Night-Soil Men* (Salt, 2024), and *There's No 'F' In Wonderful* (Salt, 2025). His collection of short stories, *In This Block There Lives a Slag… And Other Yorkshire Fables* (HarperCollins, 2001), won the PEN/Macmillan Silver Pen Award in 2002.

ABOUT THE CONTRIBUTORS

David Barnett is a journalist, novelist and comic book writer based in Bradford. After many years working in regional newspapers, he became a full-time freelance writer in 2015, and as a journalist works primarily for the UK press. He is also the author of several published novels, including the bestselling *Calling Major Tom*, and writes comics for DC, IDW and others.

Becky Cherriman is a Yorkshire-based writer, educator, performer and facilitator. She is the author of a poetry pamphlet, *Echolocation* (Mother's Milk), and a collection, *Empires of Clay* (Cinnamon Press). Her work has been named in the Women's Poetry and Women's Poets' Competition, Fish Short Story Prize, Ilkley Literature Festival Open Mic, and the Forward Prize. Since 2003, she has creatively collaborated with communities, individuals and artists, including nine years of co-leading the Ilkley Young Writers and Bradford Young Writers groups. She is currently writing memoir with support from an Arts Council England Developing Your Creative Practice grant, and is Writer-in-Residence for the Methodist Modern Art Collection as part of Bradford 2025 UK City of Culture.

Sairish Hussain was born and raised in Bradford. She studied English Language and Literature at the University of Huddersfield and progressed onto an MA in Creative Writing. Sairish completed her PhD in 2019 after being awarded the university's Vice-Chancellor's Scholarship. Her debut novel, *The Family Tree*, was published by HarperCollins and shortlisted for the Costa First Novel Award, the Portico Prize and The Diverse Book Awards.

Marcia Hutchinson was born in Manningham, Bradford, the seventh of nine children to Windrush generation Jamaican parents. The first pupil from her school to go to Oxford, Marcia worked as a lawyer before returning to the North and founding the educational publishing company Primary

Colours. She was awarded an MBE in 2011 for her services to Cultural Diversity. Now a full-time writer and member of the Black Writers' Guild, Marcia's solo literary debut, *The Mercy Step* (Cassava Republic), was published in July 2025.

Abda Khan is a lawyer-turned-writer and author of the novels *Stained* (2016), *Razia* (2019), and the poetry collection *Losing Battles Winning Wars* (2023). She is currently working on her first historical book inspired by her late father's service in World War II as part of the Punjab Regiment who fought alongside British soldiers in Burma. Her work has also featured in various anthologies and publications. She writes commissioned pieces (short stories, scripts, poetry), delivers creative writing courses, and produces and directs her own creative community projects.

Lesley McEvoy was born and raised in Yorkshire and has had a passion for writing in one form or another all her life. However, the writing took a backseat as she developed her career as a behavioural analyst/profiler and psychotherapist – setting up her own consultancy business and therapy practice. Deciding in 2017 to focus on her writing again, Lesley's debut novel was *The Murder Mile* (2019), followed by *The Killing Song* (2021).

Saima Mir is an award-winning journalist and writer. She has written for *The Guardian, The Times, The Independent* and *The Daily Telegraph*, and worked for the BBC. Her work appeared in the anthology *It's Not About the Burqa* in 2019, and *The Best Most Awful Job* in 2020. Her debut novel, *The Khan* (Point Blank, 2021), was shortlisted for the Crimefest Specsavers Debut Crime Novel Award, and longlisted for the Jhalak and Portico Prize. Saima is a recipient of The Commonwealth Broadcast Association World View Award and The K Blundell Trust Award. Saima's work has been longlisted for The SI Leeds Literary Prize and The Bath Novel Award.

ABOUT THE CONTRIBUTORS

Ross Raisin is the author of three novels: *A Natural*, *Waterline*, and *God's Own Country*. His work has won and been shortlisted for over ten literary awards. He won the *Sunday Times* Young Writer of the Year award in 2009, and in 2013 was named on Granta's once-a-decade Best of Young British Novelists list. He has written short stories for *Granta, Prospect, the Sunday Times, Esquire,* BBC Radio 3 and 4, among others, and in 2018 published a book for the *Read This* series, on the practice of fiction writing: *Read This if you Want to be a Great Writer*. Ross teaches creative writing at Goldsmiths University and is a writer-in-residence for the education charity First Story.

Marjorie 'Malachi' Whitaker (née Taylor) was born in 1895 in Bradford, the eighth of eleven children. On leaving school, aged thirteen, she was employed in her father's bookbinding works, wrote verse for greetings cards and an unpublished memoir. In 1917 she married Leonard Whitaker, who was then in the army, and for the next few years moved about with him. In the mid-1920s she started to publish short stories in magazines: her first collection *Frost in April* was published in 1929, followed by three more: *No Luggage?* (1930), *Five for Silver* (1932), and *Honeymoon and Other Stories* (1934). In 1939 she published a memoir, *And So Did I*, but after that wrote very little. She died in 1976. A selection of her stories, *The Journey Home and Other Stories,* was reissued by Persephone Books in 2017.

Special Thanks

The publishers would like to thank Bradford 2025 UK City of Culture, Valerie Waterhouse, Francesca Beauman at Persephone Books, Abi Fellows at DHH Literary Agency, Dionne Hood at Bradford Libraries, and Olivia Chapman at Word Up North.